A

COLLECTION

OF

CHRISTMAS

SHORT

STORIES

A

COLLECTION

OF

CHRISTMAS

SHORT

STORIES

Compiled by Lorna J Child and Peter Hopkins

ENCHANTED FOREST PUBLISHING LTD.

First published December 2020 by

ENCHANTED FOREST PUBLISHING LTD.

27 Old Gloucester Street,

London,

WC1N 3AX

United Kingdom

www.enchantedforestpublishingltd.com

A CIP catalogue record for this book is available from the British Library.

ISBN: 978-1-8383322-0-4

We did it!

Our very first Christmas book, and we could not have done it without everyone's support.

We want to say a HUGE thank you to everyone who submitted their stories and got published in Enchanted Forest Publishing Ltd. first book…

A COLLECTION OF CHRISTMAS SHORT STORIES.

Thank you to Max and Jason from Fire Fm, for chatting to myself (Lorna J Child) about it on radio, then submitting your own (rather cheeky) Christmas poem 'Santa's Bulging Sack'.

A very special thank you to Ryan Wilce, (placements officer of Plymouth university, English and creative department) for being just as excited about this project as we got the ball rolling and helped organise us a team of University students to help with the book.

You are all amazing, and we are so excited about working together more with the Plymouth University students as we are sure many will become talented writers in their own right.

iv

We hope you enjoy the book and we wish you all (including you the readers) a very Merry Christmas!

Lorna J Child and Peter Hopkins

Enchanted Forest Publishing Ltd.

www.enchantedforestpublishingltd.com

THANK YOU

CONTENTS

A FRIEND AT LAST

by *Lorna J Child*

24th December 1902

I t had snowed continuously for several days now. Bitter cold winds cruelly whipped the faces of those who were brave enough to venture outdoors for last minute Christmas gifts for their loved ones, those fortunate enough to have money to spend that is.

Cheerful, excited children, dressed in their finest fur coats and warm mittens, gazed wide eyed at the toys they wished for, for Christmas. Men in top hats, and women in beautiful dresses, admired what the market stalls had to offer.

A group of carol singers stood with their hymn books, singing 'O Come, All Ye Faithful' whilst happy onlookers joined in with the words that they were familiar with, and the joy of Christmas radiated throughout the privileged crowds.

A little way off from the busy market stalls, stood a little girl with long blonde curly hair, dressed entirely in rags, and no shoes on her feet. Her age I'm unsure of, maybe 8 or 9, but I know her name was Clara, she adored Christmas, and loved nothing more than to see people smiling. She walked barefoot across the snow towards the carol singers, and found herself singing along, her voice just like that of an angel. When the song ended, and the crowds cheered, the little girl walked off towards a busy lake, which was quite frozen now by the sudden drop in temperature. families cheerfully skated, laughing as they went. The older girls spun gracefully round, whilst boys raced around, competing with one another. Clara liked watching the skaters and wished very much that she could do that.

Suddenly a snowball brushed past Clara's face. She turned to see a young group of children, similar in age to Clara, throwing snowballs at each other.

"Hey!" cried Clara smiling, but the naughty children ran off continuing to throw snowballs at people passing by.

Higher up on the hill, Clara saw three young girls. They were busy building a snowman. Clara watched with fascination.

"May I join in?" She asked one of the girls, but she barged past Clara in such an aggressive manner, completely ignoring her request. Clara felt the warmth of her coat brush past her cold skin, and for a moment wondered what it would be like, to wear a coat just like that one. How fine she would look, Clara thought to herself.

The sky grew darker, and soon the busy town diminished in numbers. Clara made her way up the hill, towards the forest, where she went every night. A place she felt safe and lay down behind the trees. She gazed up at the night sky, and said her prayers, before falling asleep.

It had just gone 11pm, when Clara was woken up by a young couple, who walked by giggling to themselves. She sat upright nervously, and was just about to lay back down again, when she spotted the snowman across the field, sparkling under the moonlight. It seemed to twinkle like magic. Clara realised this would be the only moment she would have the snowman to herself, and bravely walked across the thick snow, across the field. Clara gasped as she realised the snowman's nose had fallen off. She picked the carrot up and put it back into position on his face.

"There you go sir, much better!"

She said, smiling at the sparkly snowman, and was just about to turn around, when the snowman answered her back.

"Thank you, missy," he replied.

Clara's mouth dropped open in surprise

"Did you just say that?" She asked

The snowman looked into Clara's eyes,

"I believe so missy, yes."

A tear formed in Clara's eyes.

"It's been a very long time since anyway spoke to me."

"Oh," replied the snowman, "I hope I didn't offend you in any way."

Clara smiled. "Of course not," she answered back.

The snowman was curious to know where all the children had gone that helped to make him. Clara told him how they'd gone home, to prepare for Christmas, and the little snowman wondered if he should go home, to prepare for Christmas too.

Clara wanted to show him where the people lived, and delighted by her offer, the two walked off hand in hand across the snow-covered fields, down to the town where the people had disappeared too. Peeking into one of the windows of a very grand house, Clara saw a young boy, hanging a stocking up by a glorious fireplace. His mother helping him and smiling as she did.

"Father Christmas brings presents to all the good children." Clara told the snowman, who was watching with intense fascination.

"It looks so warm and cosy inside" said the little snowman, "and just look at their beautiful Christmas tree, so sparkly and..."

Suddenly a howling wind blasted down the narrow street, pushing the snowman down to the ground, and a blizzard of snow temporarily disturbed his vision. When it calmed, the snowman looked up, the little girl was nowhere to be seen.

"Clara?" The snowman called, running along the street to find her. He eventually spotted her, standing outside a small church.

"How did you get here so fast?" He asked her, slightly out of breath.

"I don't know," she replied, "It's funny… sometimes I feel like I'm in a continuous dream… is that strange?"

The snowman thought for a moment

"No," he replied, "I don't think that it is?"

They stood silent for a moment and listened. Inside the church, voices could be heard.

"What's that lovely sound?" Asked the snowman.

"Singing!" replied Clara, "isn't it beautiful"

Inside the well-lit church, a choir sang "O Holy Night" and the little snowman and Clara both stood side by side and listened, then Clara started to sing. The snowman began to cry, he'd never heard anything so lovely before. He couldn't take his eyes off her, and suddenly felt a feeling of love for his new friend. Neither he nor Clara noticed he had begun to melt.

They walked across the empty high street, back towards the field. The snowman looked at the frozen lake.

"What's this?" he asked, as he stepped onto the ice.

"Careful!" Clara cried, "it's very slippery, I wouldn't want you to fall."

But the snowman giggled as he slid perfectly across the frozen lake.

"Join me," he said, coming back to take Clara's hand.

Clara bravely joined him on the ice. She looked up at the snowman and smiled

"May I have this dance?" The snowman asked.

Clara giggled. "Why sir I'd be delighted," and she gave him a curtsy. The snowman then began to sing her, her favourite song "O Holy Night", he knew every word, and sang it perfectly.

They danced together gracefully, smiling all the while. The snowman whispered in Clara's ear.

"I wish we could stay like this forever."

"Me too," Clara whispered as he spun her around under his arm. He pulled her close again.

"Be my friend forever."

Just then the world seemed to spin. Clara looked up at the snowman

"A friend?" she asked

The snowman looked confused.

"Yes, we're friends aren't we. You like me, and I love you!"

Then Clara remembered something she'd long forgotten.

"I always wanted a friend, I never had one, but no one could ever see me."

The snowman looked puzzled at Clara. Then suddenly a bright golden light shot down from the stars, and a beautiful angel appeared from above them. Clara looked up, "Mumma!" she called excitedly.

It had been so long since she'd seen her mother, she'd quite forgotten what she looked like.

The angel came down and extended a hand to Clara. The snowman suddenly realised that Clara was going to leave the earth forever.

"No!" He screamed, and as he screamed, he began to melt even more, "Don't leave me" he begged, "I'd rather die than be without you." And he began to cry.

Clara, who had remained on this earth for many years after her passing, had wanted one thing before she left, a friend, and this darling snowman had been more friendly to her than anyone had ever been. She smiled and took the snowman's hand, and together the three of them left the silent snow-covered earth, to be together forever, in heaven.

FORGETTING DECEMBER

by Keiran Potter

The dust lay like sheets of snow on every surface. Undisturbed by years of absent feet. Kay rested a cardboard box spilling with books and a handful of childhood memories on her hip. A medal from that time she came second in the 100m sprint, a reading certificate with her name in fine line black.

She flicked on the hallway light and sighed. The moving van wouldn't be arriving until at least Tuesday, so that meant she'd probably be sleeping on the floor and eating nothing but dry bread and crisps until then. She swung the box from her hip and placed it on the hard wood floor of the living room. For a second she considered the prospect of forging a hammock from a decade's worth of karate belts. Her mother always said they'd come in handy, but Kay doubted whether that this is what she had had in mind.

Outside the snow flurried in swift rings as if dancing with the wind. Kay had always loved snow as a kid. But these days it reminded her of ash, sitting on lampposts and collecting in the part of her hair.

It had been two months since the fire that stole her childhood home in the dead of night. But somehow, she could still smell the soot in her hair. She still checked her tissue paper every time she sneezed to see if it was stained with the remnants of coal.

December had brought in the harsh winds. The memories clung to the gusts, plastering themselves on every window-pane that Kay turned to.

The staircase greeted her feet with an orchestra of muffled groans. Kay found if she walked on her toes, the creaking was easier to avoid, so she crept up the stairs. A ballerina pirouetting through a harmless minefield.

The bedrooms were as bare as the rooms downstairs. One had a window that stretched the length of its side wall. It framed the sweeping forest that lay below, like the finest painting. Only this one seemed to breath. The snow streaming in great ropes, peppering the conifers with silver crowns. Kay presumed that the second room was perhaps a nursery or something, its size and lack of windows being her main tell.

As Kay closed the bedroom door and began across the landing and towards the stairs, she felt something prick her cheek. She wiped her face with the back of her hand but only saw a smudge of damp where a droplet may have been. Above her was the loft hatch, just like the one back at her old house. Except this one may have been flaking paint and splintering at the edges, but it was not yet a pile of ash as hers had been. That was a relief in itself.

Through the troughs in the rotting wood of the hatch, Kay could see small twinkles of red and green seeping into the landing. For a second she thought she might call the police, fearing that someone may have been living in the attic for all the time the house had been empty. Then how silly she would feel, if the police would come and find nothing but cobwebs and dust. With that Kay ran down the stairs, tipping the memories from her small box and leaving them scattered across the living room like odd tombstones in a cemetery.

On the landing, she stood with her bare feet on two corners of her upturned box, spreading her weight lightly to avoid falling to the floor in a crumpled heap. She strained to reach the metal catch embedded in the wood but managed to flick it with the edge of her nail. It fell open and with it a ladder slid from its brass hinge, unfurling like the branches of some ancient, swaying tree.

The green and red was now much more vivid and cast itself across Kay's face, a dozen warm fingers. As she ventured up the ladder, a soft chuffing rhythm filled her ears. Her head popped through the hatch and she considered turning back, closing the hatch and pretending that this had never happened. But her wonder kept her head floating in the loft space, bobbing like a toy ship that couldn't believe its eyes.

A miniature steam train puffed in loops around the loft hatch, shimmering in gold and dripping with scarlet gems. It blew smoke into Kay's face and raced off again, disappearing behind the trunk of a vibrant conifer. She'd never seen anything like it, the wood of the tree split off at its roots and surged through the floorboards. Kay couldn't tell where the tree ended and the floor began, the two had bled into one another from years of wrestling.

The tree felt familiar, but Kay struggled to place it. It was a snapshot from a memory that was never hers. When she was a child Kay's grandmother had spoken of a time where December was full of grand trees and lights that shone like a million burning stars. Presents wrapped in an abundance of bows.

Like a birthday but for everyone. All on one day. They called it Christmas.

They had banned Christmas decades ago, the same year that organised religion was outlawed. The move had cracked the country right open and left many fleeing for freedom. People chopped trees in the middle of the night and stowed them out of sight come day. Those who were caught could have been arrested.

But that government had collapsed years before, yet Christmas had remained lost amongst the cinders.

So, Kay sat in the lap of the tree and watched the train splutter and spit. As she did, she noticed that ash tumbled through broken roof tiles and collected in her hair. She touched it and it fell away into the air like glitter.

No. It wasn't ash.

It looked like snow.

THE BEST GIFT

by Aimee Whittle

She wandered alone through the crowded shopping centre on Christmas Eve. Light shone through windows filled with gifts, topped in red hats and tinsel.

The captured smiles of strangers looked down on her from the walls as she walked, an imaginary sparkle placed carefully on their teeth. Decorations cascaded from the ceiling in bright metallic colours; lights glittered around them like raindrops frozen in time.

A distant, jolly voice danced out of the speakers, followed by sleigh bells and piano keys. It bounced off the walls, echoes racing down the rows of last-minute shoppers. The smell of pork drizzled with apple sauce lingered in the air as someone passed by, biting into their bap from the Hog Roast stall outside.

She watched as people darted in and out of shops, desperate to find that one pair of slippers that Aunt Julie had asked for, or that specific pot of roasted nuts that Grandad liked.

One little girl begged her mum for that nice stuffed teddy over there – it was only £10 – and said that it didn't matter if she knew about it, it could still be a surprise.

The escalator was fast approaching, and she stepped onto it. There was no one in front of her, but she stuck to her step the whole way down. The young man behind got impatient, striding past her down the stairs and out the doors of the shopping centre. She followed soon after.

The night air was crisp, and her thin coat did little to keep out the wind. She looked longingly through some glass at a mannequin wrapped in a scarf, envying the neck that had never felt the cold. People walked by her, arm in arm, laughing together. A couple, gloved hands entwined in a single coat pocket. A man with a baby wrapped up like a burrito in a pram.

Her eyes stung now, from the breeze, and she blew her nose before it could drip. Chilly air always made it drip. She stopped briefly outside a shop with a leather handbag in the window. The slightly glossed, cream colour looked like liquid. It was displayed on a stand covered in tumbling waves of black velvet. There was a small, golden label on the front.

The small express supermarket wasn't as busy as she thought it would be. She headed straight for the meat section. They were out of chicken.

"Aren't there any in the back?"

"No, I'm sorry Miss. They go very quickly this time of year." The assistant looked sorry, but she knew he didn't really care.

The wine section was almost empty, but she managed to grab a cheap bottle of red. And a box of chocolate. He liked chocolate. The self-service queue was long, so she went to one of the manned checkouts.

"I'm sorry, the transaction didn't go through. Do you want to try it again?" The young girl at the till reset the card machine, waiting as she reinserted her card.

"It's been declined," the accusation came. Heat flooded her face as she felt the stares of the people behind her, their eyes burrowing into her head.

"I'll just take the wine," she replied, every fibre of her being on fire.

He would like the wine more than the chocolate, anyway. The till-girl rang up the wine from scratch. The receipt was printed and handed to her without a word. She left as quickly as she could.

Outside, she stuffed the bottle with its receipt into her tattered denim shoulder-bag. The top of it stuck out. In her mind, she defended herself against accusations of alcoholism from people she had never seen before and would never see again. She walked briskly back to the car, straight past the outdoor Christmas market where the little huts bordered with felt snow sat happily underneath the starry sky, surrounded by a halo of warm lights.

It was a long walk to the car. She had managed to find a free space in a neighbourhood close to town. She could see it, just up the road ahead. But shadows hid the branch that snaked out of the bushes at the side of the pavement. It grabbed hold of her bag, and with one fierce tug ripped it from her shoulder, tearing the strap. She knew she should've got that new one last week at the charity shop. She caught the bag, but watched as the wine bottle slipped into the air, crashing to the ground and sending pieces of broken glass flying in all directions. Her jeans were painted red. She stared for a moment at the glint of the moon in the fresh pool, before moving slowly to her car and driving home. The radio played Christmas tunes as she sat in silence.

When she opened the door, she stepped on a letter, leaving a vaguely red mark. She saw her name in print, bold and unforgiving, and placed it in the growing pile with the others.

She wanted to go straight to bed, but she could see light creeping underneath the door to the living room. She opened it wearily, then froze. Fairy lights, twinkling in every corner of the room; candles, placed perfectly upon the table; rose petals, littering the floor; a mistletoe, hung precariously from the ceiling lamp.

17

He stood by the fireplace, adjusting some tinsel and humming to himself.

"What's this?" She asked. He spun around, terror rewriting his face.

"No, no, no! You're not supposed to see!" He rushed over, trying to usher her out.

But, realising it was too late, he gave up.

"It's for you," he smiled broadly.

"But," her voice cracked, "but I didn't buy you anything." She could feel the tears creeping to the edges of her eyes, threatening to jump from her lids.

"It doesn't matter, you've got me the best gift of all," he said, taking her hand. She searched his face for answers.

"Your time is the most valuable gift in the world."

STRIP MALL SANTA

by Donovan Smith & Philip Rogers

S leigh bells jingled as the last customer left the store for the night and headed out into an infinite sea of white. People were in a hurry to join their loved ones and spend the night together by the fireside, enjoying the magic of the holiday season. The store was wrapped in tinsel with red and green lights. There was a giant silver tree over by the shoe department where a drunken man in a Santa costume had sat, bouncing kids on his lap and hollering "Ho, ho, ho," as though he actually believed he was the reincarnation of jolly old St. Nick himself.

I locked the door and took a deep breath, exhaling all the stress of the last-minute Christmas Eve shoppers from my body, and for a moment everything returned to normal. As I stood there, I felt calm and at ease, knowing I would soon be home with my two beautiful boys. There was nothing on earth I wanted more than to see their lovely little faces sparkle as they opened the presents Santa had brought them.

Suddenly, a loud bang went off behind my head, snapping me out of my trance. I turned around just in time to see snow sliding down the front windows, followed by the sound of giggling children.

"Get out of here you little shits," I screamed, caught off guard by their juvenile prank.

This time of year always gave me the creeps and I hated closing the store all by myself, but as the senior assistant manager I didn't have a choice. With around forty minutes until the clock struck midnight, I snapped it into high gear and began counting the tills, putting the slips and money in the safe. If I hurried now, I could still make it home with a few hours to spare.

After double checking everything, I put on my coat, gloves and was about to grab my bag, when the phone started to ring. Hesitant to answer, I picked up the receiver and spoke, "Thank you for calling Mellow Coast Department Store. This is Emily. How may I help you?"

A couple seconds of silence went by and I was about to hang up, when a loud, heavy panting came over the line, like some sicko was pleasuring himself on the other end. It began to get faster and more perverse and I screamed into the phone, "Who is this? What do you want? I'm going to call the police!" Furious and frightened, I slammed the phone down and jumped back.

Just as my feet finally touched the floor, there was a series of rapid booms, and I freaked. Scared out of my mind,

I snatched up my keys and ran for the exit. I punched the bar on the back door and rushed to my car, looking back over my shoulder the entire way.

There was a crunching sound behind me, causing me to fumble my keys, as I desperately scrambled to get inside before things got worse. Glancing back, I saw the same drunken Santa from earlier tonight, making a beeline right for me. His eyes were cold, dead and I could tell by his body language that whatever his intentions, it didn't look good.

Drool was foaming from his mouth, and he had a crowbar in one hand and a brown paper bag special in the other. He was stumbling and yelling incoherently, and I just wanted to get out of there as fast as possible. Without thinking, I threw the car in reverse and spun the tires until I heard a loud thump. Something had collided with the side of my car.

Out of nowhere the man reappeared, the white beard, red suit, and big black boots moving frantically as he began to yell, banging his fists on the hood. He kept repeating something over and over, but I couldn't make it out. I shoved the gear into drive and gave it everything it had. I could see him screaming in the rear view as he disappeared under the veil of night.

Just as I was home free, the car began to shake violently and I hit the breaks, bringing me to a complete stop. I knew

I had only driven about fifty feet and was scared the strip mall Santa was still out there lurking in the shadows.

And just like that, there he was again, banging on my window, speaking in tongues.

"Go away," I cried. "Just leave me alone."

"Lady, I'm yus tryna tell you ya got a flat," he slurred.

"Just go away," I screamed. "Please don't hurt me!"

"I'm not gonna hurt ya, I'm only tryna help yous you stupid bitch," he screamed back. "You don't want my help, then fine. Freeze your ass off out yere then for all I care."

"Leave me alone," I cried, "I'm going to call the police!"

As I sat there for a few minutes, wiping tears from my face, waiting until the coast was clear, I remembered the present my daddy had given me the year before. A three-inch engraved pocket-knife with my name on it.

With no one around, I opened the door and hopped out to get a better look. Just as I did, he appeared out of nowhere from the rear of my car and started to yell, spit flying from his mouth like a filthy, disease infested rat.

"Please don't kill me," I have a family! I have two kids, please!" I held the knife out and the closer he got, the more I swung it out in front of me, fearing for my life.

"Get away from me," I said. "I don't want to die."

"Die," he said, a bit confused. "I'm only trying to help you lady."

As he reached out and grabbed me by the wrist, I jammed the tip of the blade deep into his neck. Blood squirted as I pushed it in further and repeated the action a few more times, just for good measure of course. I finished changing the tire and then stacked him on top of the other body in the trunk of the car. The boys were going to have a good Christmas this year, I had a good feeling.

"You strip mall Santa's are all the same," I said, flicking the lighter as I closed the trunk.

I slid behind the wheel and turned on the radio.

"That's right folks," said the DJ, "Lock your doors, keep your eyes peeled, and be safe tonight. The Strip Mall Slasher is still on the loose."

IN THE EYE OF THE BEHOLDER

by Georgie Young

It dawned hot and bright, a crystal blue sky void of interruption. She'd slept with the window open to let in the ocean breeze, but it wouldn't be long before she had to close it firmly against the stiff Sydney heat.

Down at Coogee Beach, it was like any other day. Runners trotted the coastal path in groups and pairs, Mums with prams bought lattes and banana bread at beachside cafes. Colourful towels dotted the rich, amber sand whose grains were the texture of coarsely ground coffee. Caitlin dropped her towel in a puddle upon them and tucked her keys into one of its folds.

Hot limbs cut through brisk cold water as she dove into the waveless bay, the salt sending a tonic- like dry tickle to the back of her throat. After a few idle strokes, she rolled onto her back to float, drinking in a moment's peaceful reflection before the rest of the day arrived. Around her, the chatter of the seagulls mingled with the vibration of the heat that was to come, while the windless backdrop let the disparate voices blur into a hum.

She dropped into Maggie's for a quick morning coffee on her way home, and so that her nieces and nephew could show her their swag.

"Look, Aunty, look what I got," India cried, dressed in an orange, striped bathing suit and brandishing what appeared to be Elsa gloves and a wand. "I'm a princess," she shrieked, twirling with the clumsy elegance of a four-year-old who already had her daily sugar consumption well and truly covered.

"She's going to be out like a light before lunch is served," Maggie observed. "It's going to be a damn sauna at Mum's today, can you put the clamshell in the car on the way out?"

She hadn't understood the significance of being someone's aunt until India had come along, she mused while loading the plastic wading pool into the back of the hybrid that stood wilting in the driveway next to a thirsty-looking lawn. For one's own children, sure, but for her sister's? It was unexpectedly rewarding.

Caitlin arrived freshly showered, in a white cotton summer dress that hung loosely below her breastbone and would sufficiently hide any indulgences in Aunty Pat's passionfruit trifle and fruit mince pies.

"There you are, darling," her Mum blustered down the hall to greet her. "Everyone's in the back and your Dad's just warming up the barbecue." She took the green salad that Caitlin was holding and pressed a lipsticked kiss to her cheek. "You look lovely, darling. So fresh and summery."

Maggie was standing at the island bench in the kitchen taking cling wrap and aluminium foil off an assortment of mismatched dishes. Beyond her, the living room gave way to the timber deck and a stretch of unkempt garden. The venetian blinds were at half mast, enough to cast light but discourage its radiant heat. The rhythmic tick of the ceiling fans clicked overhead.

"Can you take these two out to the others," Maggie said by way of greeting, handing her a bowl of potato chips and a platter of dip and bright orange carrot sticks. "Victor's already complaining about being hungry and lord knows we'll all pay if he has too many beers on an empty stomach." Victor was Maggie's father-in-law, and with not much other family to speak of, had been adopted into theirs.

Caitlin stepped through the sliding door that led to the deck and approached the fan of family members that hovered near the barbecue. She met their chorus of greetings with a bright, sun-ridden smile and accepted a sweaty kiss from her father, who lifted his white panama hat as he bent towards her.

Aunty Pat offered her a choice between a home brewed punch and a glass of bubbles, and she accepted the latter, knowing that anything brewed by Aunty Pat required a stout constitution ill-suited to the makeup of the day.

Maggie appeared bearing a platter of fresh oysters and prawns arranged around a bowl of lemon wedges. They flocked, like the seagulls at Coogee beach, and Caitlin relished the wash of the ocean as it slithered down her throat. The kids opted to stick with the potato chips, and returned to running around under the sprinkler set up expressly for their diversion.

Later, after they'd filled themselves with sausages and cold ham and every salad under the sun, stuffed in a last mouthful of fruit cake and brandy cream, they dispersed to various corners of the house. The kids napped in the upstairs bedroom, their cheeks beet-red with the heat and the crusted remnants of candy canes. Her Dad ushered Victor, Rob and Aunty Pat into the study to check the team line ups for the cricket the following day. Her Mum and Maggie left the sink full of dishes and rewarded themselves with an afternoon Pimms to wash away the dessert.

"Come join us," Maggie called, gesturing to the pitcher beside her.

"In a minute," Caitlin said.

She found a patch of shade in the garden and threw a ball for the dog to chase half-heartedly. She lay on the grass and listened to the echoes of similar events across the hundreds of backyards holding thousands of families just like hers, across the city.

Eventually they drew back together, emerging from their respective corners to congregate around the pitcher of Pimms and nibble hesitantly at the assortment of leftovers, to the relief of the overflowing fridge. The kids, rubbing sleep from their eyes, started their gentle but persistent chorus of 'when are we leaving', to the chagrin of the fading will of their parents.

"Soon, my dearest," Maggie whispered, pressing her lips to the side of India's head.

Caitlin opted to walk home in the fading dusk with a full stomach and a container of potato salad tucked under her arm. Barefoot and content, relishing the sting gone out of the day.

Another Christmas Day done right.

DESULTORY MEMORIES OF CHRISTMAS IN ALUM ROCK

by John Roberts

I had a dream last night, I'm not sure if its real, if it's how it was, how I imagined it to be, or a composite of dreams, part forgotten, part imagination, part make believe, but this is what I dreamt.

Oh, those innocent long time ago days. I remember the Christmas it snowed. The smell of paraffin, it was all over the place, lingering like a low-lying persistent engrained mist, in shops, mates' homes, everywhere.

On Christmas Eve morning, we wuz' playin' in the cul-de-sac. We three Davy Crockett fur-capped adventurers, me, Philip Stevenson Sidney Hartopp, with school friends Stanley and Clive, building snowmen using cast off coal for eyes and carrot tops as noses. And snowball fighting with each other, it was all the rage in Clodeshall road that Winter. Wrapped in coats, with excited eyes, frozen feet that crunched upon white snow. Homemade kitted gloves, balaclavas, scarves, dressed in shorts with our socks pulled up only a little bit of leg showing. Hands wet, fingers icy cold and red Rudolph the reindeer noses. Out hot breaths blowing out more fiercely than any Walt Disney Dragon.

I do recall old Mrs. Roach, who lived alone with lots of cats, at number ninety-nine, came out handing out biscuits and cakes. Phillip gave me and Sidney a Jammie Dodger and wandered away.

Sid turned and whispered, "eh, don't you think these biscuits taste a bit icky sweet…odd…I think I can smell cats on em." He lisped the letter 'S' when saying sweet and smell," I reckon her moggy has done a whoopsie on em' eh."

Later on, that star filled and dark, bitter frosty Christmas evening, the five of us went carol singing. Singing snatches of songs, badly, discordant, but rewarded with pats on the head and sausage rolls, hot sausage rolls.

Christmas was the festival of lights. The walls festooned with greetings cards, Holly, balloons, and handmade decorations made at school. With a real Christmas Tree standing in the corner of our postage size living room, and I mean small. The tree decorated with coloured lights, I think, its branches bowed with baubles old and new, a Robin and an angel. Dad used to pick up my sister to proudly place the angel upon the top of the tree.

On Christmas Eve, at bedtime, Mom and Dad would lay out a plate with a mince pie and sherry for Father Christmas. Dad playing Bing Crosby 's 'White Christmas 'record constantly, Mom busy cooking in her small broom cupboard sized kitchen. Going to bed in the evening, us three lying wide awake in bed whispering about longed long presents. Christmas morning, we made patterns in frost on the inside of the windows with our fingers.

Christmas day morning, up at the crack of dawn, we'd find stockings hanging beside our beds, holding a mandarin orange, walnut, a coin, puzzle books and an annual. I remember my Mom watch us open our gifts, a big smile across her happy face. Neither Mom or Dad knew Christmas, as you and I do, lived it through us and loved every Moment.

Dad used to open the door between the front room and lounge with a real coal burning fire alight in the front room. The turkey came with all the trimmings, sausages, bread sauce and stuffing. Roast potatoes, mashed potatoes, carrots, parsnips and of course, sprouts. For afters, jelly, mince pies, custard, and Christmas pud with silver sixpences. Pride of place on the table the Christmas cake, covered in icing, decorated with Father Christmas a snowman and a sprig of holly. Afterwards we would watch Morecambe and Wise, stupid TV shows and Cliff Richard.

I recall the bells of the Rosary Catholic Church booming out all Christmas day and the stream of men and women, boys and girls sauntering to and from Mass, often by way of 'The Country Girl' and The Rosary Irish men's club. A protracted line of worshipers, sinners and Borstal boys wishing friends, neighbours, relations a Merry Christmas and other such seasonal homilies.

The Rosary club found in the bowels of the Catholic school seemed to my young eyes strange and exotic, smelling of aromatic incense and alcohol the walls a fading magnolia colour. The peeling paintwork hidden by strategically located wooden crosses and various colourful prints of Mary, Christ and his Disciples portrayed in mock baroque style full of long lingering enigmatic stares.

In the evening, the club would be a fog thick full of Woodbine cigarettes and Gold Block tobacco coupled with the aromas of Davenport's beer, Jameson's whiskey, and Guinness. At closing time, the more inebriated drinkers and wannabe singers would break into heart rendering songs of their old country and variations upon rebel melodies.

In the late afternoon, after the Pubs closed, we would receive visits from masses and masses of people passing through wishing everyone happy Christmas. It was an open house, there were uncles and aunts and friends of varying shapes, sizes, and associations, relations by birth, relations by marriage, suggestion, and tenuous connection. Several escaping wife, family, or in-laws. One or two dodging the false seasonal bonhomie, others sort of waifs and strays, the lost, lonely, wayward, and confused who sought a moment of sanctuary and love, if only temporary.

You could always pick out the hangers - on drinking friends, with swollen red Pinocchio noses and broke into songs, warbling drunkenly, and off tune, a mix of carols and latest pop ballads, the lyrics becoming more ribald as the night wore on. They usually ended up asleep snoring in a corner chair until late evening when they were unceremoniously turfed out by fellow drinkers and the more sober guests.

The world seemed a more innocent place than now. Even the Milkman and Postmen delivered on Christmas morning. Ordinary delivery men, always Men in those days, who knocked on doors with blue frozen knuckled fingers and warm smiles.

A SHORT CHRISTMAS TALE

by James Farrington-Tillyer

I

There was a month left until Christmas. Alfred had not seen or heard from his son Garry for months. He was aware they were both at fault and neither of them were to set in their ways change now. Garry lived nearby but his wife Amy and step-son Joshua consumed most of his spare time. Alfred did not begrudge this, he was exactly the same way at Garry's age.

It was six am in the morning when Alfred heard his white cat Simon scratching at the door. He knew what would happen if he didn't get up from previous experience, so he put on his blue and white dressing gown and slipped into his Burgundy slippers and made the journey down the stairs to let Simon out. He would never have described it as a journey when he was younger but in his twilight years getting out of his bed was something that he had come to consider an achievement. He gave Simon a stroke on the head and Simon reciprocated by rubbing his nose into Alfred's hand. Alfred opened the door and watched Simon bounce out into the cold. He noticed for the first time since the spring the water vapour from his mouth. Winter was finally here, he thought to himself.

II

It was now only a week left until Christmas. Garry and the family had arranged to come and see him in the afternoon on Christmas Day. As usual he couldn't remember who sent the first text to open the conversation, but he was looking forward to the company. These past few weeks he was alone. When he had let him out that first cold morning weeks ago, he had not returned. This had happened before in short periods, but never this long. Alfred however had seen most of his friends, family and pets come and go over the years so had begrudgingly accepted that he was now the sole occupier of his house.

It was time to prepare for Alfred opened his back door and headed into his garden. The patio used to be covered in pots full of beautiful plants but was now just covered in pots full of soil. It was his beloved wife who lovingly crafted the garden. He always appreciated it when he'd sneak a peek out of his kitchen window, but now she was gone he didn't have the desire or skill to maintain it. He took his old spade out of the shed and headed to the bottom of the garden. There was a row of Christmas trees planted in a row. They were memories from when Garry was younger. Every year they would go to the local garden centre to visit Santa Clause. A small present and a small Christmas tree would be the prize after what seemed an eternity waiting in line. After Christmas, before Alfred returned to work, and after the small presents were forgotten, he and Garry would go to the garden and plant the small tree.

When he arrived at the collection of Christmas trees, he realised they were no longer that small. There was only one small enough that he was going to be able to remove from the ground. His favourite, the last one from before Garry stopped believing. A memory of a more innocent time.

In the evening, after several hours of hard work, the tree was decorated in his living room next to the fire, where they had always placed the Christmas tree. Luckily the other ritual from when Garry was younger of having to retrieve the decorations from the loft had no longer had to happen as now It was only Alfred in the house, they only made it as far as the spare room when they were last packed away.

III

It was now the evening on Christmas Day. Alfred was in his chair next to his simmering fire. He put his empty glass back on his coffee table then picked up his half full bottle of whiskey. He removed the cork and poured himself another double shots worth of whiskey into his glass. He replaced the cork then placed the bottle back onto the table. Garry hadn't managed to visit in the end, but they did manage to have a fifteen-minute conversation on the phone. He was content with that, they'd see each other in the new year. Maybe this new year, maybe next new year he laughed to himself. He would just have to put up with feeling alone til then.

At least he had his sandwiches to look forward to tomorrow, he thought to himself. They were made from the leftover Turkey from the Christmas meal with a healthy amount of cranberry sauce. They was something that reminded him of his wife that he did have the skill to continue. He felt himself slowly drifting off. There was no reason not to.

There was a faint noise. Alfred started two wake up. It took what seemed minutes but was probably only seconds for him to come to terms with the fact that he wasn't in his bed. The noise got louder. There was someone at the door. "Hold on, hold on. I'm coming." Alfred shouted. He put on his blue and white dressing gown and slipped into his Burgundy slippers and made the journey to the door. He took the key from the side, put it in the door and turned it. Next he pulled down on the handle and swung the door open. A less white, skinnier Simon came running in, stopped, sat down and looked at Alfred.

There goes the leftovers for my sandwiches, thought Alfred. He wasn't upset by that at all.

THE SELFIE

by Dean Jarvis

December is a wonderful month. It's the one time of the year that I actually get to come out.

The other eleven months are all about people; annoying, intrusive, the whole lot of them. They're always strolling about my backyard. Every day is the same. No one cares about my privacy, always trying to get that elusive photo shot of me.

Last week, I caught one of them with fake shoes on, trying to make footprints in the snow. Do they really think I'm a size nineteen?

A few days later, I saw some idiot running around with a Yeti suit on; his accomplice was filming him. To make matters worse, they were making Yeti calls with a musical instrument. For your information, I don't sound like a yak.

The worst thing about these fraudsters is, they bring in the crowds.

Yes, I know the town is called 'Bigfoot' for a reason and that's how our local community makes a living, but jeez, it can get a bit much sometimes.

Now as much as I hate the crowds, Christmas is indeed a good time for me. Around this time, my town has scores of publicity events going on. It's basically alive with people dressed up in Yeti suits. Last year alone there were over thirty fake Yetis walking around.

Christmas allows me to venture into the city, to have a bit of a walkabout.

Once there, I stop over at Santa's grotto. For the measly sum of ten bucks, you can get your picture taken with a friendly Yeti.

The guy who runs the place is always late to open up. I think he has a slight drinking problem. I take advantage of this and pose with a few early tourists. I like the Japanese ones the most. They call me 'The Hairy Godzilla' and are big tippers.

After getting paid, I visit the local shopping mart.

I pick up a raspberry Swiss roll and a couple of packets of Monster Munch crisps; cheese and onion flavour, my favourite.

I then take a mosey on down the high street. En route, people stop and stare, saying, 'Wow! That costume looks so real.' I normally give them the thumbs up and keep on walking.

With all that, I am heading back to my den. Tomorrow, I have relatives visiting. There is an ice-rink in town. I am considering a family outing.

Christmas is the one time of the year that makes me feel all warm and fuzzy on the inside.

Right, back to my to-do-list before the relatives arrive, I'm making my special brewed cherry eggnog this year.

THE CHRISTMAS TATTOO

by Louise Nulty

K evin zipped the paper from the printer, collected his Christmas jumper, and headed out. "Yes mate, got it. It's sick. People are gonna think we're mental. Can't wait to show everyone at the Christmas do tonight."

"Great, see you in five."

Alfie met Kevin outside of the tattoo parlour. The window was surrounded by twinkling Christmas lights and displayed a strange mixture of tattoo art and random antique-looking oddities.

"This place looks mint."

"Yeah, the artists here are great," Said Alfie, who had chosen this studio. If he was getting a tattoo, it was going to at least be done properly. Kevin's judgement was questionable at best, given that most of his tattoos were selected while he was utterly wasted.

"Let's see it then," Alfie asked. Kevin brandished the folded piece of paper like it was a wad of banknotes. Alfie tried to grab it, but Kevin deftly swiped it away.

"Ah, ah. I lost the bet because of you, so you have to get the same design as me, and I'm getting this." He said, waving the paper.

"Fine." Alfie huffed.

The inside of the tattoo parlour was much like the window display. They sat on two red velvet cinema seats and waited. A slim man in a tweed waistcoat, covered with tattoos and impressive facial hair, called them over to the desk.

"So, what design are you thinking?" He asked.

Kevin laid out the piece of printer paper with as much reverence as a pirate might unfurl a treasure map and pointed excitedly at the design.

"A Christmas Tree?!" Said Alfie, genuinely surprised that it wasn't something obnoxious and Kevin-like. Kevin was known to have an assortment of ridiculous tattoos, not to mention a long list of girls' names up his forearms, each with a strike-through.

"Where'd you get this?" the artist asked, turning the page, noting the web address.

"Found it online, thought it was cool. Goes with our jumpers, see?" he said, unveiling a hideous Christmas jumper, complete with a cheeky Santa losing his pants on a rooftop.

"Right." the artist said. "Y'know this website does occult stuff; Voodoo, witchcraft? Those symbols around it might mean something. Are you sure you want that on your body? I could still do a cool Christmas piece, just without the symbols. Protect your...soul or something?"

"No way. I want it even more now," said Kevin.

"You sure? You shouldn't mess with this stuff, you know?"

"Yep. Two of those, please, Garçon," he said, jabbing at the page.

Alfie had made the sensible decision to have a small version on his forearm. He had foregone the potentially satanic symbols in favour of a Scandinavian style tree and wolf silhouette. He knew he wouldn't hear the end of it from Kevin, but quite frankly, it was a permanent fixture on his body, and he had to, at least, like it. Kevin stepped into the waiting area rubbing his chest, sticking the dressing tape down. *It's massive.* Alfie thought, inwardly rolling his eyes.

"The others are in the Welly," Alfie told him on their way out.

The next morning, feeling a mighty throb in his head and still considerably intoxicated, Kevin switched off his alarm and moved to the bathroom, searching for water. After chugging a pint, he examined the tattoo in the mirror. A prickle caught the back of his throat, making him wretch and cough violently. Something sharp was poking him.

Reaching his fingers into his mouth, he drew it out in painful, prickly tugs. It was a small Fir tree branch, covered in bloody spittle.

"What the hell? What was I doing last night?" Feeling too disgusting to rattle his brain further, Kevin returned to bed to sleep it off.

His phone buzzed again some hours later, his headache much improved, but the memory of the branch was still a mystery.

"Alright mate?" Alfie said, "You alive?"

"Just. I must've been completely smashed. Did I eat a Christmas tree last night? Found some twigs."

"What? Not that I know of. Anyway, fancy a few on Christmas Eve?"

"Yes mate; just gotta get over this one first."

The rest of Kevin's day remained uneventful; he lounged about recovering with box-sets and takeaway pizza; that was until the itching started. First on one shin, then the other, then his arms, then everywhere. He became so irritated that he decided to take a shower.

Drying off, he felt the towel snag on what appeared to be a splinter in his forearm. Pinching it, he pulled a zigzagging branch out of his arm like pulling a worm from the ground. Kevin's hysteria grew as he spotted more of the branches just below the surface. Looking down at his legs in horror, he saw his skin had sloughed off, revealing dark ridges beneath. It was on his arms too, his neck, everywhere. He called Alfie and his mum, panicking, leaving garbled voicemails.

On Boxing Day, Alfie made the decision to go to Kevin's flat. He hadn't shown up on Christmas Eve or returned any calls or messages. It wasn't entirely unusual, particularly if he had met a girl and holed himself up for a week, but the incoherent voicemail on Alfie's phone was worrying.

Using the spare key 'hidden' under the mat, Alfie let himself in, pushing hard against the door; something was blocking it.

A Christmas tree with branches out-stretched took up most of the hallway.

"Why is that there?"

After a quick search, Alfie found Kevin's phone, keys, and wallet. Concerned, he decided to call the police and Kevin's mum.

Something's wrong.

On his way out, he battled once more with the tree, this time noticing the ornaments. A red one had the name Stacey with a strike-through it, another Olivia. In fact, there were many girls' name ornaments interspersed with golden symbols that Alfie seemed to recognise from the tattoo design, and the fairy on top wore an obnoxious Christmas jumper.

LAST CHRISTMAS

by Yausan Ward

'Good morning. And it looks like sunshine and showers are on the table for Winter Holiday Day....'

Margaret turned away from the TV. So, not quite bikini weather but much warmer than the December days of her youth. Back then December was cold and frosty, even snow if you were lucky (or unlucky depending on your point of view). You wore woolly hats and scarves, warm coats and boots. But global warming came and stayed so it was now T shirts and shorts, sun hats and sunglasses.

And Winter Holiday Day. Margaret shuddered. The Americans started the change by calling Christmas Happy Holidays. People used to wish Merry Christmas to each other until the Christ part was thought to insult non-Christians and the Merry would infringe the rights of those who had mental issues. So Merry Christmas was banned and wishing each other a Good Winter Holiday was now the norm.

The computer beeped. She clicked on this, that and the other and her son's face appeared on the screen.

'Morning mum. How are you? Looking forward to Winter Holiday?'

'It's just me and you, dear. You can say "Christmas" to me. I won't tell.'

Her son shifted slightly in his seat and looked behind him. Then he leaned conspiratorially towards the screen and whispered:

'So are you looking forward to Christmas mum?'

Margaret smiled at him and nodded.

'I'm sorry we couldn't afford a Covid secure hotel for us this year for the Winter Holiday. The prices went sky high after that outbreak in the spring. The kids and Joanne are really disappointed that we can't be together this year.'

'I'll miss being with you all, but I won't miss that stuff they put in the air in those places. It might kill any Covid that people bring in and stops anyone catching it from anyone else but it smells and it tastes horrible. It ruined Christmas (her son looked wary as she said the C word) dinner for me and every other meal as well. Even makes the alcohol taste funny! I'm sure that stuff tarnishes the decorations, rusts anything metal and kills the trees.'

'It's safe mum. They wouldn't want to kill off the trees. These trees are going to save us. They use up all the carbon dioxide in the atmosphere. So you have a tree in your home for the Winter Holiday and then afterwards, it gets replanted outside. Don't worry, I'll sort out the replanting for you. Did they deliver the decorations as well?'

She nodded and sighed. Decorations were now made of recyclable or natural materials such as wood, glass and metal and were expensive, so much so it was cheaper to hire them for the festive season. Glitter and paint were banned as were decorations made of man-made materials. She missed her old tree decorations. Her old tree decorations...

'Mum, have you got something *Christmassy* for your dinner tomorrow? I could still sort something out if you haven't.'

'Don't you worry about me. You and Joanne and the kids enjoy your jackfruit turkey and Quorn chipolatas, as much as you can. It's a shame that the real stuff costs so much today. I hate being forced to be vegan.'

Her son shrugged.

'I know but it's supposed to save the us and the planet. Less animals on the planet, less carbon dioxide being produced and less carbon dioxide will kill off the Covid. And then we can all meet up in each other's homes again says the Prime Minister.'

He did not look convinced.

Margaret wasn't convinced either. The Government may say they were following the science, but she did not believe that global warming and Covid 19 were linked, that the greenhouse gases in the atmosphere were somehow mutating the virus constantly so that it always one step ahead of mankind. Someone somewhere would be making money out of this notion.

'Right mum, I'll call tomorrow. You take care now. Love you.'

'Love you too.' And he was gone.

Margaret climbed up into her attic. After some rummaging around, looking into this box and that, she found what she was looking for and carefully carried it downstairs to the tree.

They were still bright and as beautiful as the last time they were hung on a Christmas tree. Gilded opulent fruit baubles in red and gold. White and silver angels. Little painted bells. A figure of Father Christmas. Plastic holly with red berries. A tiny flat Christmas tree, made of dough and baked hard, clumsily painted green with a sprinkle of glitter and with her son's name written in a childish hand still on its back. Margaret put them all on the tree, relishing every law-breaking moment.

The turkey was brining nicely in the garage. She had the bacon and the chipolatas in the fridge ready for the tomorrow. She would bake her favourite cake tonight and she had made herself a little sherry trifle too. All that meat, butter, eggs and double cream had cost her two months of pension and it had been hard. But, as she put her hand to her breast and felt the insidious little lump there, she intended to enjoy Christmas as much as she could the way it was meant to be enjoyed.

After all, it would be her last Christmas.

A CHRISTMAS SURPRISE

by David Hayes

The doorbell rang. Dad got up from the kitchen table. Mum remained seated and anxiously murmured "fingers crossed!". Accompanied by his daughter Sarah, Dad returned – his arm around her shoulder. Sarah spoke first. "Unfortunately, I didn't get the part." Mum stood up and hugged her daughter. Sarah continued: "It's okay … of course I'm disappointed, but I'm delighted for Anna …my bestie deserves it. And may I remind you – again – that both of you have pointed out that coping with a disappointment is always the first step in taking on the next challenge. One setback will not ruin my Christmas. And, anyway, all my classmates and I are looking forward to the Zoom performance … we'll all be famous."

"I must say, Sarah, you're taking this decision in your stride," remarked Dad, proudly.

Sarah's reply – "Well, Dad, I am a very mature ten-year-old after all" – introduced a moment of laughter. "Now Mum, if you're going to the nursing home to see Gran, I'll go with you."

"That's very thoughtful of you, pet. Gran loves your company … give me five minutes."

Sarah's grandmother has been a long-time resident in the nursing home. Due to almost-complete memory loss, she has forgotten all family names. The three-generation family bond manifests itself mainly in the exchange of smiles between Gran and Sarah who is Gran's youngest grandchild.

Sarah's mother, in particular, treasures this special relationship.

SIX WEEKS LATER

The community room in the nursing home was packed to the capacity allowed by COVID-19 restrictions during the Christmas period. The residents' Christmas concert – which is the seasonal musical highlight – was held over three successive nights this year. The Christmas tree, lights and decorations provided a marvellous setting – and the atmosphere was electric. The socially-distanced-marked dance floor was alive with a mix of *Strictly Come Dancing* and *X-Factor* wannabes of all ages. To everybody's delight, the musicians – dressed as Santa and his elves – played all the old favourites. There was one hiccup, however. The band leader apologised for the absence of one particular band member whose rendition of *O Holy Night* had always been much anticipated and greatly appreciated. The groans of disappointment spread throughout the room.

"I wonder", continued the band leader, "if anyone here would like to sing that carol." Sarah's parents looked at their daughter and nodded. Sarah thought about it – momentarily – and then volunteered to much cheering and clapping.

This carol was Gran's all-time favourite. Sarah had sung it six weeks previously at her school's audition, and now she wanted to sing it especially for Gran. A standing ovation told its own story as loud applause and requests for an encore rang out. Needless to say, the performance went viral – and Sarah was invited back to perform on the following two nights ... much to her parents' delight.

Later, back in Gran's bedroom, Sarah and her parents were saying and waving their goodbyes. Unexpectedly, Gran beckoned Sarah to her bedside. Holding Sarah's gloved hand, Gran beckoned her own daughter as well ... and firmly held her gloved hand, too. Touching moments, indeed! But what followed was the icing on the Christmas cake.

"Kathleen," whispered Gran, "Sarah was brilliant ... I even sang along with her ... my favourite carol. She's got a beautiful voice – it's as good as your own."

In an instant, Sarah and her parents were gobsmacked and overcome with wondrous emotion. Listening to Gran's reaction to Sarah's singing was their best ever Christmas surprise. And this bedroom scene went viral, too – thanks to Dad, again. It was, indeed, the happiest of nights for the family and for the nursing home staff. In the words of another hit song, *Oh, what a night*!

A KRAKATOA CHRISTMAS

by Beverley Byrne

My new boyfriend Derek was joining us for Christmas. Auntie Mu, the family matriarch, always travelled up from Merthyr to ensure traditions, like lunch being served dead on one o'clock, were obeyed like the Ten Commandments. 'Does that mean I can't go to the pub,' bleated Derek. 'I always have a drink with the lads Christmas morning.'

'Look Derek, you'll be doing me a massive favour. My smarmy brother's always been Auntie's favourite and having competition will really piss him off.'

'What's she like then?

'A Welsh version of Vlad the Impaler.'

On the day, Auntie's lips compressed like a vice as Derek forked aside the turkey.

'Vegetarian you say. Not in this house.'

Refusing Auntie's 'special trifle' didn't go down well either. 'That recipe, young man, has been handed down the Llewellyn female line for generations.'

Derek's gift, a bottle of sherry, remained unopened. 'Thank you but Lucy might have mentioned, as a member of our local Chapel, I never take alcohol.' Derek shot me a wounded look and mouthed 'thanks' behind her back. After lunch and the Queen's speech, 'We always stand for the National Anthem Derek', Auntie stepped up interrogations. 'So Derek, just how lucrative is stand up comedy? Let me know when you say something funny and I'll do what I can.' In the end, Derek waved the white flag and got stuck into the sherry while my brother smirked over his third helping of trifle.

When Mum suggested a game of Trivial Pursuits, my heart sank to my reindeer embellished slippers. Convention decreed Auntie could take as long as she liked to answer a question, even when it was about football or Pop music, her Gobi Desert of ignorance in an otherwise fact filled brain. Being wrong was not in Auntie's DNA.

Long silences, interrupted by mum asking if we wanted 'another mince pie' or 'cup of tea', stretched into festive infinity.

Shifting uncomfortably in our dead father's chair, Derek topped up his glass while Auntie gazed at the ceiling rose, saying, 'I'm sure I've heard this on Eggheads.' Finally, the Krakatoa moment. Derek, who'd been staring miserably into the fire while Auntie pursed her lips and blew out rosy cheeks in endless contemplation suddenly stood up and said, 'For Christ's sake Auntie, give it up. Of course you don't know Dizzee Rascal's real name. Nobody bloody does. I'm off to the pub.'

After the front door slammed, Auntie gave me her disappointed face and said, 'I'm not too keen on your young man Lucy. Surely you could do better.' As it turned out, Auntie was dead right about that.

THE BELL

by David Woods

It hung, all brass and ornate gilding, in the frozen tower that wept icicles. There was no movement. Below, the rising commotion from the town streets heralded the beginning of the final, frantic Christmas Eve activities. The bell had nothing to add. The church had been closed in November for renovations which had taken longer than expected and so the toll of goodwill was left absent from the season.

Stress from the growing throng of shoppers sounded out, pushing up against the silent church walls and the tower. The bell absorbed the shouts and calls, the desperate hunts for last-minute bargains and the right kind of trimmings for the turkey dinner. An emaciated Santa called out season's greetings, his own handheld bell tinny and apathetic. The bell took it all in, motionless on its mount.

The morning overflowed into the tumult of midday. The shops surrounding the church greedily swallowed up customers before spewing them back out, never learning from their indulgence. Carrier bags were locked in tight grips, white-knuckle rides carried on waves of triumph back to the multi-storey car park in the centre of town. Car horns blared and lines of traffic were formed on the roads leading in and out of town, lying in static formation like unused tinsel.

A tramp broke away from the crowd, approaching the church yard gate. He moved in a lop-sided shuffle, chugging at a can of ale that was updated for the season in festive artwork. Pushing through the gate, the tramp headed for the bench on the side of the path leading up to the church entrance, the only quiet spot amidst the bustle where a person could make merry. The tramp sat down heavily with a groan and refreshed his palate with another swig from his can, switching his bleary gaze from the thronging shoppers to the scaffolding propped forlornly against the church walls.

His eyes ran up the metal poles and wooden boards until they reached the bell hanging silently in its tower. A strange sense of otherworldly wonder gripped at the tramp and he let his jaw drop slightly, letting the pervasive cold hold the drops of beer on his beard, which was the same colour as the murky-grey sky above. He thought it was a shame the bell would not ring on its big day, that Christmas had no call to offer than angry voices and the throttled coughs of vehicles.

As he marvelled at the bell's refined design, the tramp let out a ferocious belch, set off by his latest slug from his can, a bit more prolonged than the rest. The belch travelled upwards as the tramp put a hand across his mouth in needless embarrassment and, whether it was the force of the expression or the sudden charge of wind that met it at the tower, the bell was disturbed, finally, from its slumber. One deep, solitary peel rang out as the bell swung on its cradle before falling back into its starting position.

The echo of the chime seemed to be exponential and did not have a seeming end. The tramp listened, staring in awe at the bell as he did so, to the sound that announced the season in such grandeur. He turned to survey the crush of shoppers, searching their faces for signs that they recognised the call to cheer and celebration. And perhaps somewhere, as the echoing chime passed across reddened faces to complaining, chapped lips, there was a sign something would be taken home that didn't have to be wrapped, cooked or left in the attic until the next December festivities.

TINY SNAPSHOTS OF YOU

by Georgia Cook

In my family, Christmas is all about the tree. We're a well-travelled bunch, hailing from all over the globe, so holiday get-togethers can be a logistical nightmare. But the tree...the tree will always be special.

My Mother started collecting ornaments when I was five years old, the year my older brother Jamie left for university. He was moving away to Edinburgh, and I remember our Mum taking him very sternly by the sleeve before he left.

"Send me back an ornament," she said. "The brightest, gaudiest ornament you can find. That's how I'll know where you are. That's how I'll know you're enjoying yourself."

She was delighted when, two months later, a package arrived on our doorstep from Jamie. Inside, neatly wrapped in red tissue paper, was a tiny set of tartan bagpipes, festooned with holly. My mother hung them pride of place on our Christmas tree, and just like that the collection was born.

Every year afterwards, no matter where we went, my mother

demanded we send her back a Christmas ornament. She received glass snowflakes from Cornwall, festive felt penguins from Canada, a tiny clay dolphin from my uncle in Barbados. When I was seven years old, I sent her a glittery pinecone from my first weekend at camp; handmade in the crafts tent with extreme concentration. It was hung carefully at the top of the tree upon my return, its bristles glinting among the branches, and I'd never felt so proud.

Soon my mother's Christmas tree became a beacon of family travels; a brimming green testament to everywhere we had ever been, everything we had ever picked out for her. No matter how small, strange or tacky, it went on the tree, and my mother adored it just the same.

One November I asked her-- as we carefully unwrapped and sorted the box of ornaments, untangling lights and inspecting tinsel-- why she only asked for Christmas decorations; never postcards or knick-knacks or food. I was the youngest of five children, and I knew my siblings would gladly have sent our mum anything she wanted.

"Because these are tiny snapshots," she said, dangling a little wooden Santa (from my sister Lilith, in Russia, three years earlier) from her fingertips. "Everywhere you've ever gone, everything you've ever done, you've sent a little piece back to me, and now I keep them safe."

She hung the little Santa up on the tree, where it whirled and glittered, suspended in the air.

"It's a tree of memories; all my memories of you. And it's the gift you give me every Christmas, no matter where you go, or how you spend it."

I stared up at the tree, resplendent in its coat of tinsel and lights, hung with years of family travels and family joys-- ornaments from Morocco, Australia, London, Moscow. A tiny world of us; all my mother's children, captured over and over again in all our little moments. All our little adventures.

No matter where we were, no matter who we became, we would always be here, safe on our mother's Christmas tree.

And nothing would ever be more beautiful.

A DECEMBER TO REMEMBER

by Shaylan Levens

Eva leant up against the window in the chalet and watched the snow fall silently outside. It hardly ever snowed back home in England and she longed to get out and explore.

She had arrived in Meribel two hours ago, after finding the perfect secluded chalet, on a last-minute travel page. She didn't have any family back home and had just found out the love of her life was having an affair with her best friend. It was just too much to handle and she needed to get away. Somewhere away from all the hustle and bustle of everyday life.

Somewhere that she could just lose herself in a romantic novel in front of a log fire. It was the twenty third of December and she didn't want to spend Christmas alone, but what choice did she have and what better place to spend it, than the French Alps.

Eva was an event planner from a little village in the south of England called Stonevale. She loved her job but in a strange way this was actually a welcome break. It was only 6pm but it was already dark outside and the view out of the window was like something from a film. The orange glow of the lights bounced off the glistening snow-capped trees all the way down the valley and Eva felt a million miles away from everything going on back home.

She then realised she hadn't picked up anything for dinner, so she tied her long brunette hair into a messy bun, grabbed her knitted earmuffs and coat and headed to the front door, but as she approached it, she could hear some dogs barking and a French accent muttering something. Suddenly there was a loud knock. Eva opened the door and her emerald eyes lit up, she was greeted by a burly man with a short dark brown beard 'bonjour madame je suis Theo' the man replied. 'Hi, I'm Eva' - The man must have noticed that she didn't speak French and luckily started talking in English. 'Did you lose something this evening he questioned, 'as I've just found a little black bag up there' and he pointed up towards the path.

'There are only two chalets up here so I thought it must be yours, I know it's not mine' he laughed. 'I live just through those trees with my daughter lily' He showed Eva the bag 'Oh my goodness that is mine' She said quite shocked ' I only arrived a few hours ago I must have dropped it by mistake, Thank you so much!! I can't believe I didn't notice!? Let me make you a drink to say thanks!' she replied. 'No don't worry it's fine I'm just glad you got it back, but if you're free tomorrow evening, lily is going to be with her mum, so we could have a drink together. My friend owns the bar just over the valley and we could ski down?'

'I don't actually ski' Eva said shyly. 'You don't ski!!? Well if you would be up for it we can take the huskies down'

'What do you mean, take them down?? ' Eva questioned. 'I own a sledging business, these are 2 of the huskies, the rest of the pack are back at the chalet.' He explained to her.

'What a great job, that sounds like a perfect evening, I'd love to' Eva said excitedly.

'Great I look forward to it, I'll pick you up at 7pm tomorrow?' he told her.

The next day Eva woke up to the sun shining through the wooden blinds in the small but beautifully furnished chalet and she couldn't stop thinking about meeting Theo the night before. It felt strange that it was already Christmas Eve but she was excited to spend the evening with him and wondered what the night would bring.

Eva couldn't believe how much happier she was feeling and decided that she would go out and buy a small Christmas tree to put up.

She grabbed her red coat and handbag, then headed out in search of the perfect tree.

By coincidence about 10 minutes down the snowy lane there was a sign for Christmas trees, so she followed it round the bend and picked a small spruce tree. There was a small quirky handmade stall at the front of the tree cabin selling decorations, so she picked out a dozen or so pretty red and silver embellished baubles and a gorgeous crystal star to go on top. There was also a beautiful hand painted ceramic husky dog, with little beads for eyes and she thought it was perfect.

Next to the tree cabin there was also a little cafe and artisan chocolate shop so Eva thought it would be rude not to go and have a look. The display in the window was so enchanting, there was an elegant Christmas scene all made out of chocolate. A tall dark chocolate Christmas tree took centre stage with ruby chocolate baubles adorning each branch.

Intricate milk chocolate chalets had been carved and surrounded the tree, along with a white chocolate snowman complete with scarf and top hat. It was so charming, she just had to go inside. There was a glass counter stretching the length of one side of the shop and there were shelves filled with every type of chocolate truffle you could think of. The colours were just breathtaking. Each one had been delicately finished with different toppings, lashings of gold leaf, rich ganache, vibrant pistachios, salted caramel discs and praline to name a few.

Eva chose a hand wrapped box of four truffles to give to Theo later that night and headed back to put the tree up.

When Eva had made it back to the chalet, she put the little tree in the lounge by the fireplace and attached the ornaments to each branch. She carefully placed the crystal star on the top and stepped back to admire her creation. It looked magical.

The day had passed so quickly and it was nearly 5.30pm. Eva had time to get in the outdoor hot tub before she needed to get ready to go on the husky ride. She poured herself a glass of prosecco and slipped into the bubbly paradise. This was a fantastic way to unwind from the day, she would never tire of the view and wished it would never end. After a long soak she got changed into some blue Jeans and a thick burgundy jumper. Then she brushed her hair and put on her favourite cream bobble hat.

Theo turned up on time at 7pm with the sledge and huskies. 'Hi Eva! Are you ready?' he said. ' Yes, I can't wait' she said excitedly. 'It will take about 25 minutes to get there, I will take you past the frozen lake and hopefully we will see some roe deer and possibly a marmot or two' explained Theo. Then he passed her a soft blanket 'Here, put this around you, it gets quite cold when the dogs are pulling it at speed.'

'Thank you, I'm really looking forward to this.' Grinned Eva. She carefully stepped into the sledge and wrapped the blanket around her shoulders. Theo sat in next to her and Eva could feel the warmth of his arm against hers. As the Huskies pulled the sledge through the snow, Theo and Eva chatted as if they had known each other for years and soon they came to a small clearing and the sledge slowly came to a halt. Right there in the moon light, stood three elegant roe deer with a distinctive white patch near their tails. They stood so still in the crisp air, until the dogs pulled them again and the deer ran back into the forest. 'Ohh Theo, watching them there was really special.' Eva whispered and he smiled at her.

The sledge went past the magnificent lake and as they glided past, the moonlight reflected off the ice like a glittering diamond.

If Eva could have taken a picture then she would have. As they headed back into the forest, Eva saw the huskies make a sharp turn around a large fir tree and then felt the sledge shudder and suddenly they launched into the air.

Eva rubbed her eyes and rolled over and as she looked around she realised she was in her bedroom back at home. It was all a dream. Eva closed her eyes again to try to take her back to that moment but it wouldn't work. She was already awake and as she sat up in bed, her husband Theo was next to her sleeping soundly and their dachshund lily jumped up onto the bed excitedly. What a strange but wonderful start to Christmas day...

THE BEST CHRISTMAS PRESENT OF ALL

by Joseph Arechavala

I could only see the faintest glimmer of light from distant houses. The trees were thick, long rows of branches and pine needles with barely room to walk between them, and there wasn't any moon to guide us. We walked right behind each other, afraid of somehow losing our way as though we were out in the middle of the forest. There weren't any stars out in this cold night, and our breath made frosty clouds in the air as we huffed along our way. The shack was back—that way, I think it was—somewhere.

We kept hunting for just the right tree, not too short or tall, not too spare or bushy—actually I as the one searching. Aaron's face had that look; I could tell even in the dim light. The one he wore when he was thoroughly exasperated, his eyes dark under the hood of his sweatshirt and hands jammed in his pockets. We'd been married long enough for me to know.

"Just pick one, willya?! I'm freezin' my ass off!"

"It has to be just right," I curtly responded. "This is our first Christmas with Angela."

71

He emitted a low growl. "She's not gonna know one from another. Should've gotten a damn artificial tree. We'd be home with her now decorating it and drinking eggnog instead of freezing our butts off out here."

I quietly scoffed in reply. We'd been out all day and Aaron's mood started out bad and rapidly plummeted from there. I wanted—no, scratch that—I needed everything to be perfect for our daughter's first holiday, from the decorations to the wrapping for her presents to her first Christmas dinner. Of course, once his bad attitude started, I started to get exasperated at him for getting exasperated at me…when did this go from fun to such a chore?

I sighed in resignation—then I noticed her.

She was a little ways off and I didn't pay her much attention at first. She was a very pregnant, young woman in her twenties, wearing a coat that had seen better days, seemingly searching for something other than a tree. She stumbled as I watched and caught herself on a branch of a spruce.

"Hold on," I quickly said to Aaron, and rushed up to her. "Miss, are you all right?"

"Oh thanks," she replied with a honeyed, southern drawl, her breaths rapidly making one cloud after another in the cold night air. "Y'all don't you work here, do ya? I'm lookin' for a tree."

"Uh, no, I don't. But I can help you take it back to your car if you need it. Did you decide on one?"

"Not really," she replied, looking down at the frozen ground. "These're kinda expensive. I was hopin' they had somethin' a little less...well, pricey."

I looked back at Aaron, as he examined the tree in front of him. Pulled a twenty out of my pocketbook and placed it in her hand and quietly said, "Merry Christmas."

She protested with hands waving. "Oh no, I cain't..."

I put my gloved hand on her bare one. She looked so cold, her cheeks bright red. "Yes. Yes, you can. Here," I added as I pulled off my gloves, "Take these too. You look like you're freezing."

"But..."

"Please," I pleaded, looking into her eyes. I unwrapped the scarf from my neck and placed it around hers. "I want you to have them. You probably need them more than I do. Can't let yourself catch a cold with a little one coming."

She began tearing up. "Thank you. Thank you so much. I wish I could do something for you...I'm sorry, I don't even know your name."

"Chris. And you are?"

"I'm Faye," she replied, again looking down demurely. "Thank you, Chris. I managed to buy the girls presents, but a tree was lookin' a little iffy. See, my husband—"

I smiled at her. "Then twenty won't be enough." I pulled out three more twenties from my purse and gave them to her.

"Oh, Chris! No, please! I cain't. It's too much. I—"

"Don't worry," I assured her as I placed the bills into her hand. "It's fine. We have plenty. And this is the time of year to share."

"Oh, no, but—"

"I insist." I grasped her hands firmly in mine.

She cried full blown now, a huge smile on her reddened, tear-streaked face. "Thank you. I'll never forget you, Chris. Thank you so much."

"You're welcome. And Merry Christmas."

"Oh, to you too." She gave me a big hug.

I left her there and went back to my husband, glancing up at the inky black sky and whispering silent thanks.

"What was all that about?" he asked with a touch of irritation.

"Nothing. Let's get a tree and go."

"Well, which one?" he asked with hands outstretched and more irritation in his voice.

I smiled and kissed his cheek, letting my lips linger a moment or two. "Doesn't matter. Any tree'll be fine. This one."

I picked it up and headed back to the front to pay for it, smiling to myself as Aaron stood completely befuddled.

OF CHRISTMAS PAST

by Christopher Joyce

Evelyn and Christian had come a long way these last few years, but Christmas was still hard for them. Just making it to their early thirties alive was something their respective families had not expected, given the addictions they had struggled with since their teens. Clean now, gainfully employed, and heading down a better, more hopeful road, they had a great deal to be thankful for. No accomplishment nor milestone, however, could fill the void in their lives which had opened the day they had given little Noel up for adoption.

They could not have kept him, not in the state they were in; still only kids themselves, hooked on drugs, and well-known to the Police, raising a child was simply out of the question. Giving up their baby, whilst undoubtedly the right thing to do, had led them deeper still into their vices as they struggled to process their experiences. Ultimately though, the very act which had caused them to spiral had also been their salvation, as each passing year chipped away at their juvenile delinquent personas to reveal the caring, thoughtful adults they had hoped to one day become.

As was their tradition, they had settled early on Christmas eve, dressed in new pyjamas and matching novelty slippers. Warmed in equal parts by the open fire at their backs and the mulled wine in their hands, they would each select one small present from the pile to open, before they would inevitably enjoy another glass or two of the hot, spicy drink and then retire to bed, "so we don't disturb Santa" as Evelyn always said.

Their routine was much like that of a thousand other couples out there, but one thing perhaps unique to them was the ritual of pouring a third glass for Noel, and leaving it on the mantle until Christmas morning, when Christian would quietly take it away and pour it out while Evelyn watched on with glistening eyes.

Three glasses poured, and the present selection process well underway, Evelyn and Christian's smiles turned to frowns as they heard a knock at the front door. Their families long-since estranged, they shared a momentary look of confusion before Evelyn stood up to answer the knocking. *Carol singers, great,* she thought, opening the door in her Santa Claus PJs and elf slippers. A teenage boy and girl in festive scarves, jumpers, and woolly hats were all smiles as they begun without preamble.

"Ding dong merrily on high…." Evelyn had to hand it to them, they could hold a tune.

"…Hosanna in excelsis!" they eventually finished.

"Yay, well done! That was great, you two!" said Evelyn, smiling and clapping. "I don't have any money to give you, but here…" she said, handing them each a Christmas cracker and a mince pie from the hallway table.

"Thanks so much, ma'am" the young girl said in response.

"Yeah, really, you didn't have to; we sing for Jesus, not for reward." added the boy. "Oh, well, in that case: God bless you. Merry Christmas!"

Evelyn closed the door and went back inside to her Husband, who was squeezing and shaking presents in an attempt to discern their mysterious contents. "They gone?" he asked.

"Be nice! I think they were from the Church; nice kids".

Evelyn had knelt down next to Christian and resumed the present picking, when another knock at the door had her on her feet again.

What now? she thought, approaching the door. Opening it, she beheld the same carol singing boy from moments earlier.

"I'm so, so sorry, ma'am, I really hate to have to ask, but is there any chance I could quickly use your bathroom? It's a long way back to the Church Hall…"

Evelyn would not ordinarily entertain the idea, but he seemed like such a wholesome young man; and he really *did* look like he was about to burst.

"Well, it *is* Christmas. Come on in - what was your name?"

"Oh, thank you, thank you so much. And it's Luke, like in the Bible. My friend's name is actually Mary, if you can believe that" he added, smiling.

"Just down the hall and to your right, Luke".

Christian's outstretched arms and raised eyebrows were met with a stern look from Evelyn, immediately forestalling his protest.

"Be. Nice." she whispered.

A few minutes later, Luke returned to the living room looking *relieved*, to say the least.

"Better?" Christian asked.

"Oh yes, much! Thank you, sir." replied the boy, making no effort to leave, but instead looking around the festively decorated living room.

"This is a lovely house you guys have here" he said, earnestly.

"Oh, thank you Luke. We like it." Evelyn replied.

"Nice place to raise a family; do you guys have kids?"

"No, no kids."

"Oh, that's too bad. Maybe one day, huh, Evelyn?" Luke said, smiling.

Evelyn and Christian felt a simultaneous chill at the back of their necks.

"How do you know my name? Do we know each other?" she asked.

"Hm? No, you must have told me." the boy replied, still smiling.

"I didn't tell you my name." said Evelyn, alarm and concern beginning to seep into her blood.

"I must have heard Christian say it then".

"How do you know *my* name? What the fuck is this? " Christian replied.

Luke stood still, unblinking, his earnest smile fading into something infinitely more malicious.

"Oh boy. Now I've done it." he said, mostly to himself.

"Where's your friend Luke; where's Mary?" Evelyn asked, suddenly concerned for the girl.

"She's gone."

"Gone where? Back to the Church?"

"No. Just gone. As a matter of fact, she's just in the alley behind your house."

"What did you do, Luke?" asked Christian.

"She was no longer useful to me, so I got rid of her. But you two would know all about that, wouldn't you?"

The boy's once wholesome face was now a mask of rage and malevolence.

"Who the fuck are you? What's going on?" demanded Christian.

"Please don't raise your voice to me, *Dad*."

Horror and disbelief etching themselves into his face, Christian studied the boy for what seemed like an eternity.

"N…. *Noel*?"

"That's right." said the boy, pulling a handgun out from under his colourful Christmas jumper and putting three bullets into his Father's chest, adding two more to his head for good measure.

"Don't you fucking move!" he screamed at a distraught Evelyn, whose fight or flight instinct had decided on the latter course of action the second she saw the Beretta.

"Why? Why are you doing this?" she managed through the tears and panic. "You made me go away." Noel responded calmly "I was an inconvenience to you, so you made me go away. Do you have any idea what it's been like for me? Did you ever even try to find me? To check in on me? The things I've…"

He stopped short. Taking a deep breath and composing himself.

"It's taken me a long time to find you" he said, and shot his mother in both legs.

Evelyn hit the deck hard, screaming, losing blood, and lying inches from her dead husband. Even without the gunshot wounds, the shock and horror of the previous few minutes would have rendered her incapable of fighting off Noel, who had now straddled her and was sitting on her chest, pinning her in place.

So distraught and frightened was she, that she did not even see him pull the knife from its sheath and only became aware of it when the cold steel blade pierced her throat in the first of many strokes to come.

The frenzied attack over, his mother and father lying dead at his feet, Noel straightened his hair and replaced his weapons. Helping himself to the conspicuous glass of mulled wine which stood alone on the mantle, Noel drank deep, savouring every drop.

Throwing the empty tumbler into the open fire, Noel cast one final look at his dead parents.

"Merry fucking Christmas."

THE HIPPO

by Abigail Wilkin

Every Tuesday, Lily and her mum visited their local library.

Lily would dash to the children's section, her eyes wide with the array of illustrated children's books.

But it wasn't just the books that Lily loved.

In the corner of the section, sat on some squashy cushions, were a group of soft toys. A crocodile with big teeth, a bear with a button nose, and a tiny rabbit with soft floppy ears.

At the centre of them all sat a hippo. Cream coloured, with two black button eyes which locked onto Lily's gaze and cast a spell over her.

While Lily's mum browsed the non-fiction section, looking for her next intellectual read, Lily escaped into the world of the toys. She hugged the hippo, read to the hippo, and laughed her heart out as she threw it above her ahead, catching the large toy as it came back down.

The library staff watched with raised eyebrows as a hippo kept appearing above the shelves in the children's section.

"Not much reading is going on over there," one of them muttered.

The weeks flew by, and Lily would eagerly ask when they were next going to the library. The highlight of her week was playing with the hippo again.

Soon October rolled into November, and Lily's parents asked her to write a Christmas list for Santa. Normally such Christmas lists would be as long as their arm, filled with requests for toys, chocolate, a bike or two, and a tin of crayons which would all disappear over the course of the next year.

This year they glanced over Lily's shoulder to read her big, wonky writing.

"Dear Santa,

A hippo please. Just like the one at the library.

Thank you. Love from, Lily."

Lily's mum glanced at her husband. This was going to be interesting - she had never seen such a distinct hippo before. Where could they get one just like it?

Her parents searched endlessly through November, asking toy shops and surfing online for a cream-coloured hippo. As the only thing on Lily's list, they desperately wanted to get it for her. If there was no hippo, her stocking would be empty.

The disappointing reply from each shop and website came back the same;

"I'm afraid we don't have a hippo like that."

Lily's mum ran a hand through her hair as she exited the largest toy shop in their town. Christmas was now only two weeks away, and if Super Toys didn't have that hippo, it was safe to say that nowhere would have it. On their next visit to the library, Lily's mum stared into those black button eyes. *You're unique, aren't you? I can't find another hippo like you for love nor money.*

As they left, Lily hugged the hippo goodbye, and her mum overhead the whispers.

"Christmas is nearly here and I've asked Santa for a hippo just like you! I'm so excited!"

A pang of guilt went through Lily's mum, needling at her heart.

That night, she complained to her husband, "I'm at my wit's end. How are we going to get this hippo? I've thought of getting other ones, but they don't look anything similar."

"Well," said Lily's dad, "there is one option."

They gave each other a look.

***

The morning broke on Christmas Day, and Lily leaped out of bed at an ungodly hour. Her parents, once roused, followed her downstairs, black circles under their eyes and still yawning.

Three fat stockings of presents in the living room brought a magical feel to the air. Lily jumped up and down with excitement, her eyes shining as she asked, "Has Santa brought a hippo?"

Lily's parents just smiled as they sank onto the sofas and watched their daughter tear off the wrapping paper of the biggest present in her stocking.

One by one, two black button eyes stared back at her. She squealed and squealed with delight, unable to believe it.

"A hippo!"

Once the hysteria subsided a good few minutes later, Lily sat with the hippo on her lap, and wondered aloud, "how did Santa manage to get a hippo just like the one at the library?"

Her mum popped a mini mince pie in her mouth and shrugged with an air of mystery. "I don't know."

But her thoughts jumped back to her visit to the library visit she'd made on her own, not many days ago.

"My daughter has asked for a hippo like the one here," she'd explained, "and I can't find one anywhere. Would you consider selling me this one, please?"

The library staff glanced at each other, quite surprised by the request. "I suppose we could. I'll check with my manager, but I don't think there will be any problem."

Lily's mum opened her purse. "How much would you like for it?"

The staff just smiled and waved a hand. "Please don't give us any. A donation to the charity fund is all we ask."

She put some money into the collection tub and walked back home with the hippo hidden in a cotton bag. Its button eyes gazed up at her the whole way back.

"Well, hippo. Welcome to your new home."

SMILE

by Hayden Parker

I looked down at the cluttered table, why am I so messy? Where's the eyeliner? On the floor, silly sod. I mean to tidy, but I can do that tomorrow before the show. My old excuse.

Jane packed up the last of her things today, we shook hands and said goodbye. It was all rather grown up, considering we'd been married for 27 years. I look in the mirror, contemplating my first Christmas alone. She'd been my rock, but also my nemesis. The bickering, the petty squabbles, all down to us not really communicating. Two lives living on different planets under one roof.

The trill sound came from the speaker in my dressing room interrupting my musings 'This is your 5 minute call'. The noise of the audience being piped through, the band tuning. Now was not my time for feigning jollity.

Rhys the company manager knocked, apologising in his usual timid way, "Are you ready Sir?". Was he intimidated by me? At 6ft 5 I tower above him, then I look down, the sight of a 25 stone man in garish make-up, in a frock that looks like a Fairy Liquid bottle would be enough to intimidate anyone, let alone a 19-year-old who could barely shave. He kept the door open for me as I squeezed through.

Standing next to rough plywood scenery, the time had come, the familiar tune from the band 'There is Nothing Like a Dame' and this is it, I walked forward and turned left, the roar of laughter hits you like a punch to the entire body, but somehow it did little to help. Words, what's the line? Inside I'm panicking, I've got six steps left to make, what's do I say? Then the audience subside and there's a deathly silence that seems to go on forever. What do I say? With the crippling light I can see figures in the front row. One little girl looks at me, our eyes lock, she can be no more than 8, clutching what looks like a rag doll, willing me to say something. Why am I so distracted, looking at the minute details? Then it just comes out, instinctively, like how the heart doesn't miss a beat. "Look at yous my luvverlies!!!" Her laugh is the only thing I can hear. Then a millisecond later a tidal wave engulfs and I start my routine.

After the curtain finally falls, I make my way back to the dressing room. 12 changes, a swollen knee (that I must phone the doctor about) and craving a cigarette that I've not touched in 8 months. Rhys is standing there by the door, looks at me, smiling and says "I can tell". I look back at him, a tear leaves my eye, he wraps his arms around me. In 6 weeks of doing this show, this is his first time he's actually spoken personally. He follows me into the room, put the kettle on instinctively, we sit and I talk. As I take off the thick coated greasepaint, I tell him about the impending divorce, the affair I'd uncovered when a show was cancelled and I went home early and the pangs of guilt spending so much time on the road, chasing after a dream of making others happy. He just looks at me all the way through, like a therapist, nodding and giving a sympathetic look. After I finish blurting it all out he says "I want to be like you one day". The tannoy squeals "Rhys to Box Office, Rhys to Box Office", he makes his apologies and leaves. Tomorrow is our final show and he's said eleven words in total not related to the production.

I will spend the night composing a letter to Rhys, giving him advice, passing on little quirks that I've been given by Dames of the past.

As I leave the theatre, there are lots of people still waiting for the 'star' in the freezing cold. He's a reality show wannabe who has trouble with shoelaces. I saw it myself, his assistant has to help him with them. They don't know who I am, probably thinking I'm some burly stagehand. Then as I make my way through them, the little girl with the doll is standing there with her rather youthful grandma. They ask for a photograph, I agree of course, getting on my sore knee to get to her height. "Smile!" says Grandma, I pull my silly face that has become my trademark. The girl introduces herself as Molly, and tells me that she wants to be an princess on the stage one day. Then it just comes out of my mouth in my Dame voice "Molly with the dolly" they both laugh. I ask grandma if they'd like to come backstage tomorrow and meet the cast. They both agree, then grandma says "Well you'd best give me your number to arrange this then" with her eyebrows raised. Cheeky grandma I thought. She passes me the phone and I put my number in.

When I get home, my first action is to grab my favourite pen, a Montblanc inscribed with the words Peter Pan - Worthing, such a kind and thoughtful gift, and start writing my thoughts for Rhys.

Then my phone bleeps with a text, it's the mysterious grandma who's name I never asked. It's Linda. I smile.

THE OLD MAN CALLED NICK WHO WAS LOST

by Samuel Skuse

I think I met Father Christmas once. It was not last Christmas or the Christmas before but the Christmas before that and I was out Christmas shopping with Mummy. I remember I was wearing my big green coat that Daddy said made me look like a pea in a pod and that always made me laugh. I lost that coat when I left it at the cinema when I went to watch Big Machines 3 for my 9th Birthday last year. We went back to find it but the cinema people said they didn't have it and Mummy said someone must have taken it. That's weird because I am quite small so either another little boy took it or a very small person took it. Anyway now there is someone else out there being a pea in a pod and that's sad because I liked being a pea in a pod. So I was out with Mummy buying Christmas presents and Mummy was getting mad because there was lots of crowds. She doesn't like crowds because it makes her feel upset and she can't breathe properly sometimes if the crowds are too big. I was holding Mummy's red coat as we moved through the crowd which I always did because I don't like holding hands. I don't like holding hands because Tim Chapman in

Year 5 buzzed my hand with a hand buzzer in school once and I didn't like it and cried until Daddy had to come and pick me up. I was holding Mummy's coat in the crowd and let go for a second because I dropped my Captain Sparks toy which was my favourite toy. I picked it up then held on to the red coat in front of me. When I came out of the crowd which took a very long time I saw that I wasn't holding Mummy's coat but another red coat which belonged to someone else. That sounds silly, but I am quite a small boy like I said before so I didn't see that it was the wrong lady. This lady looked mean and when she noticed me holding her coat she looked at me like Mummy looks at Daddy when he leaves towels on the floor. The lady told me to let go of her coat, so I did. I asked her where Mummy was so I could hold her coat instead but the mean lady was already walking off into a shop. I turned around and looked at the crowd. They were moving very fast like a river and I'm scared of rivers so I didn't want to go back into it to find Mummy. I was stood at the end of the street that had all the shops on it. The Christmas lights were hung in the air so it looked like they were floating and they were so bright that the world glowed orange and green and red. I looked around for a bit but couldn't see Mummy anywhere. I felt quite frightened then and I didn't know what to do. I was going to go into a shop but then I remembered that Mummy said not to lose her in a shop once so I was scared I would get 2x lost if I went in a shop. Then it started raining very hard and it was the icy rain that isn't snow but makes the floor slushy like a slush-puppy.

This made it even harder to look for Mummy and made me cold even though I was wearing the big green coat. I felt like crying because I was scared but then I saw my Captain Sparks toy. Captain Sparks never cries he just "gets the problem solved" which is the thing he says every episode so I decided to get this problem solved. I was getting very wet so I decided to find somewhere dry and behind me a little down the street there was a tunnel. The tunnel had a sign over it that said 'SUBWAY' so I guess it's called a SUBWAY but I don't like shouting so I'll just call it a tunnel. I ran over to the tunnel and stood inside and watched the rain drip down the entrance which reminded me of when I stood in a cave once. I was still a bit cold but I wasn't being rained on anymore so I decided that problem was solved now. I looked down the tunnel. Halfway down there was a heap on the floor that looked like a pile of blankets and some newspaper so I walked over because I thought I could use a blanket to get warm. When I got to the pile and tried to pick up one of the blankets they said "ugh what's that? Leave me alone!" with a voice that sounded like a car engine. I dropped the blanket and jumped back and said "AH" because this was a surprising thing to happen. From under the blankets a man appeared. He was a very big man with a red face and a bushy beard and small eyes that looked at me and looked angry. I stared back at him in the same way I stared at a lion at the zoo once who was also staring at me like the big man way. After staring at each other for quite a long time the man said "well, what do you want?" but not in a mean voice. I said "I lost my mummy and it's raining so I can't find her". The man looked at the rain and said "yes I can see that" then said "lost your mum you say? Well that's bad". I nodded at him and I felt like crying again but I held my Captain Sparks toy tighter. The man scratched his beard for a bit which sounded dry and looked a bit like a white pile of hay. "You should go to a shop and speak to an adult" he said, so I said "I can't because I will get 2x lost". He looked at me like I had said something weird and then he laughed quite loud which echoed down the tunnel. Then he said "okay well sit down for a sec then and we better work out a plan" so I sat next to him. He was very, very big and even though he was grumpy at first he had a kind and smiley face now. He smelled like the attic in my house which was nice because I like the attic in my house very much and it is fun to explore. He looked at me for a while then said "let me just wake up a second then I will take you find your mum". As he lifted up the blankets to sit up I saw that he had a Santa hat on the floor, which had money inside. Captain Sparks looks for clues sometimes so he can solve problems and I think maybe this was a big clue. The man said "my name's Nick" and smiled in a very friendly and nice way. I nodded as I was a bit scared still. "Now you would say your name, usually" he said, so I said "my name is Barnaby Simpkins". Nick laughed and said "very formal" which I didn't understand and then he said "well it's a pleasure to meet you Barnaby Simpkins" and shook my hand like adults do. Nick coughed loudly which seemed to come from miles down inside him and sounded like something was stuck. Then he said "you're very brave Barnaby Simpkins, bravest kid I've met in a long time" which made me very proud and I think about every day. Then he said "you'll be back with your mum in no time, alright?" and grinned so I said "okay". Then I don't really know why but I said "why are you sleeping here Nick? Are you lost as well?". He laughed again but louder this time, and then the laughter turned into coughing. He said "Yeah, something like that", did one more laugh then said "Let's go find your mum". Just then, I heard someone shout "Barnaby!" and mummy was at the entrance to the tunnel. She ran over and said "Barnaby thank god, what are you doing here?". She was so wet from the rain that it was even in her eyes. I hugged her tightly and said "it's okay mummy, I've been with Nick and he was taking me to find you". When I looked at her, I saw she was looking at Nick. It wasn't a very friendly look even though Nick was smiling at her, and Nick said "that's a very brave lad you've got there love, didn't cry once. We was just on our way to find you". Mummy didn't said anything back and held my arm and took me out of the tunnel. When I looked back I saw Nick was watching us go. Even from far away I could see he looked said, but he waved and I waved back. I thought about Nick for a long time that night, and when I told Daddy about him, he said "Hmm, do you think it was Father Christmas? Maybe he was just lost on the way to the North Pole?". Daddy knows a lot so that is probably right but also the clues I gathered make me agree with him even more. These clues are 1) The Santa beard, 2) The Santa Hat and 3) he was very kind like Santa 4) He said "something like that" when I asked if he was lost too. I thought about Nick so much that I didn't realise till a week later that I had left my Captain Sparks toy in the tunnel. Mummy took me back there after school and I was excited to see Nick again and ask him if he was Santa. But when we got there, Nick was gone. Where Nick had been, there was a page of his newspaper crumpled over something on the floor. Underneath was Captain Sparks who was standing on a note. Mummy read the note to me and it said "Property of Barnaby Simpkins, who is even braver than Captain Sparks. Merry Christmas". I never saw Nick again, I guess he found his way to the North Pole after all. But lots of people sleep in the tunnel now, different people every week. I guess they got lost too.

www.crisis.org.uk

www.shelter.org.uk

www.salvationarmy.org.uk/homelessness

SANTA'S BULGING SACK

by Jason Webster & Maxine Knight

It's the end of the year and winter is calling,

it's not long to go till the white stuff starts falling.

Santa Clause has been struggling, he's got a bad back,

because of the huge load inside his bulging sack.

"My sack is full and its weighing me down,

I can't wait to empty it when Christmas comes around".

Tasty treats for the kids are all very yummy,

the Elves even made a toy that would excite mummy.

Mrs Clause wanted to help and said,

"Come here love, why don't you have a lie down and I'll give you a rub".

Rudolph watched on with his nose shining red as Mrs Clause helped out Santa by stroking his head.

Santa felt so much better, so he got off the floor

but as it got closer to Christmas his sack bulged even more.

"How am I meant to carry teddies, bikes and these blue balls

all the way from Bournemouth, New York and Niagara falls?".

Mrs Clause couldn't believe how much his sack has grown

but at least he has his friends so he's not alone.

Dancer and Prancer, Rudolph on hand

helping relieve Santa quicker than planned.

With this size sack, the delivery could be tricky

the situation could become quite sticky.

But with the reindeers tugging him off at the speed of light

all gifts were delivered by the end of the night.

With his sack finally empty he let out a cheer

"I ho ho hope Christmas comes more than just once a year".

KINDNESS

by Julian Mercury

We didn't have a box of decorations, like I assume everyone else did. We had a, maybe, two metre long piece of green string, stretching the length from the front door to the living room. Here, we put Christmas cards: ones from the neighbours we didn't know, ones from brands Mom had bought something from only once, and some from teachers or workmates addressed to the family so as not to exclude anyone, but also to be signed and sent off in bulk. There were very few cards picked out by children my own age; the most colourful, or the most glittery, or the one with the cutest animal on the front. I remember every year in primary school I would diligently make a list of every person in my class, every person from any other class I had only spoken to maybe once, every teacher I had ever had, every teacher I hadn't had yet, classmate's parents I barely knew, classmate's siblings I only knew the name of.

I had an airtight system, recording them all from memory, recording them again alphabetically, taking my list into class with me and marking people off with the register, making sure to alternate the card types in the bulk boxes of twenty or so, signing them all in my best handwriting. I would come into class on the last day of term before the Christmas holidays, stand before the teacher, making sure their card was at the top of the pile so as to maximise the time I had to hand out everyone else's cards, reorganised into piles for each table. I would wait patiently until the end of the day, brimming with excitement to receive so many cards back, each one adding to my joy, and making me feel welcomed, accepted and liked by my peers.

I received, on average, four cards. One from my current teacher, one each from two people in my class – different people every time – and one from my friend Darren's mom, Jackie.

My grandparents had a much bigger display of Christmas cards. My Granddad had used his skills as a painter and decorator by trade to make an extending card rack, made of diagonally placed strips of wood painted green for the occasion. It was displayed proudly in the dining room, and every visitor had to look at the eye-sore every time they made the trek from the front door and straight through into the living room. All of the cards were from people my Nanna M had met a few times, or not at all, people she had spoken to at Church, Christmas themed thank you cards for her help organising the jumble sale, or just for gracing them with her presence at the Friendship Circle meeting the previous week. Everyone seemed to trip over themselves to get onto the converted Makeshift Card Rack. A few cards were even displayed on top of the fireplace, next to the Lladro ladies, and the Fabergé eggs; those were the people you know she cared about or was bragging to have received a card from.

Every time my parents took me round to visit them, there would be a new stack of coloured envelopes on her side table, next to the Wolverhampton Chronicle and a cup of hot squash, ready to be opened.

"Ah, this is from Anne at the Church. You remember Anne, Jade? Yes, you do, you do. You've met Anne. See, Jade, if you're nice to people, they'll repay that kindness back." she would say, chucking the card in a new pile for my Granddad to add to The Rack, and putting the envelope in a separate pile for us to cut the stamps out later.

Later we would go into the study where I would pull the old rocking chair up to the small table, and Nanna M could come in with a dining room chair and a special Wimbledon cushion, and we could take all the envelopes, cut the stamps out, and place them in a little box to be reused later. Then she'd bring out a biscuit tin, the ghost of a previous gift from a nameless person I had apparently met when I was small, full of tags from various presents and gift bags, and we'd spend seemingly hours crossing out all the names with non-name brand correction fluid until they were good as new and reusable again. Then I would get the special honour of selecting the boxes of chocolate or tins of biscuits from the cupboard of Things She Had Received Last Year, and chose who would be getting them this year. *If you're nice to people, they'll repay that kindness back.* If I was good, and if I had cut out the stamps well enough, I would be allowed to choose a box of chocolates or tin of biscuits to take home. I always chose the dark chocolates ones: me and my Dad don't like them, but they are my Mom's favourite.

LONELY NIGHT

by Ieuan Holt

There was no snow this December. The rain made sure of that. Its droplets wiped away any attempt made by the month to make its presence known. The landscape around the decrepit mansion was far from the picturesque scenes of the summers long ago. The fields reduced to a muddy plain whose grip could drag the most surefooted into its unknown depths. The trees like drowned men, naked, bereft of warmth, their form gnarled and disturbed from years of neglect.

He wouldn't go out today. Another violent sputter of rain upon the grand window of the parlour confirmed his decision. He marvelled at how ready they were to throw themselves into oblivion. Besides, it would be Christmas shortly and his wife and children would be arriving soon. He never celebrated the other holidays, but this one was special. He needed to move, time pressed on relentlessly in its advance and there was so much still left to do. His footsteps echoed around the empty house, each step like clockwork past its prime, as he made the required preparations for their reception.

I'll have to fetch the dogs later; the children will be so excited.

He hung the tinsel on rusted nails and rested them on dust choked windowsills, the golden hue now tarnished from years of use. The memories of his youth reared their ugly heads as he nearly lost the fight with the Christmas tree. Its greenish brown mass could've been stained red, sore lungs gasping from the retreat. He was too old, another causality of times cruelty. Yet he pressed on, the wind added its voice to his rendition of silent night, much to the disdain of the peeled wallpaper.

"Stop singing, you'll upset the dogs again," is what his wife used to say with that familiar giggle which had melted his heart, forever putty in her hands.

The rattle of the pots seemed monstrous in the devoid kitchen, the few hairs which remained frazzled in the spewing steam of the dragon like breath.

They would be here soon.

His bones cracked with the effort of setting the table. Each fork, each knife, each plate placed with military precision. The last bottle of *Massandra sherry de la Frontera,* a relic of the man he used to be was front and centre. The children's presents already wrapped and waiting; the paper torn at the corners; the little red ribbons flat and sun-bleached. Gaudy decorations hung across the dining room. Christmas crackers placed. Two for the children, one for the wife, none for him. He put up with the bangs, the smile outweighed the flinches.

No need to check the pocket watch, it was 11:59pm. So, he sat at the head, the chairs cushion deflated.

At 12:00am he closed his eyes.

He could see them all, sat around the table; his children still young, dashing around playing with the dogs. His forever beautiful wife smiled, dressed in a verdant green. The walls had a warmth in the glow of fresh candles.

"Merry Christmas," he muttered to himself, the chairs around him empty.

THE EYE OF THE FOREST

by Michaela Moclair

Behind the dense thickets of the ground and the curving bodies of the branches Evelyn spun. She spun until black dots spotted her vision and vertigo rendered her legs useless, collapsing from under themselves. She was hiding from her cousin, Vera, and had gotten side-tracked dancing in the blustery snow. Her mum had told them to play outside whilst the adults shoved stuffing into the oven and drank all the brandy. They had a small woodland attached to the back of their house and Evelyn knew every hiding spot there. She had obliged, but hid almost immediately after arriving, telling Vera to count to at least ninety-nine before trying to find her. A bitter wind contorted the spindly needles of the trees as the pigeons wiggled in their nests above. The insistent *coo, coo, coo* quiet under the sound of her breathless singing. Vera's voice came from somewhere in the distance, "Evelyn, Evelyn where are you?" Evelyn could hear her close by, she put her back to a tree.

Her mum had told her to play nice before they had left, "it's Christmas after all," she had said. But Evelyn didn't understand why that meant she had to act any different. She poked her head around the side of the tree, her breath piercing the air in puffs of smoke, and paused. But as she looked, she could see nothing, the trees formed a dense fortress either side of her. She held her breath to listen. Nothing, except the slight rustle from some unknown creature. She hoped it was a friendly rabbit.

Vera was three months younger and it wasn't like Evelyn did not like her. She did. But there was just something about her. Evelyn could hear Vera getting closer, her raggedy breath giving her away. She took her chances and ran. The trees dropped the last of their crisping leaves, guiding Evelyn towards her next hiding place.

A single branch of holly hung slightly out of reach, dangling close to the wishing well. Few red berries remained, the robins had eaten all of the rest. She paused, Vera would not find her here. Snow crunched as she used her tip-toes to pluck it, careful not to prick her finger. The berry squished in her hand immediately, spewing red juice onto her white gloves.

The wishing well had been part of the forest for as long as Evelyn could remember, a grey stoned circle with a single bucket above. Her mother used to call it the well of wisdom. At night, she told her stories of the man. The man in the well who gave you whatever knowledge you wished for. But you had to pay a price for it, wisdom was never free, her mum had said. "What did you ask the man in the well for?"

"Enough wisdom to keep you happy," her mother had said.

"And what was the price?" Her mother had told her not to worry, tucked her into bed and left, with her nightlight on dim.

Fresh snow had fallen, camouflaging the tentative shoe prints of her last visit. The well was deep, a foot of snow lining the edges, making it appear even deeper. Evelyn peered over the edge. "Evelyn, where are you?" Vera's voice came from far away, but it still made her heart race and her hands accidentally shovel a chunk of snow downwards. Vera didn't know about the well and Evelyn had wanted it to stay that way. She threw her half-squashed berry downwards. She wondered if the man in the well would appreciate it. It was Christmas after all. She had asked the man in the well many times for some knowledge. The day before, she had asked what Father Christmas would be delivering for her. Last Christmas, she had asked for something completely different.

Footsteps sounded behind her. "What are you looking at?" Vera appeared at her side, purple cheeked. Evelyn didn't know how she found her, she suspected it could have been the footprints that had given her away.

"None of your business." She looked sideways at Vera, who was staring down the well, the whites of her eyes too bright. "It's the well of wisdom," she said.

"What's so wise about it?" Vera stood on her tip-toes to peer over. She seemed taller than Evelyn remembered.

"Don't know," she paused. "I haven't quite figured it out yet." She shivered, her mum would be calling them back for Christmas dinner soon, her stomach grumbled. "You're meant to leave a gift, in exchange for a question." Vera nodded.

A voice called out in the distance, "I'm getting cold now, where are you?" Evelyn gripped onto the edge of the well, heart hammering. Evelyn looked at the figure next to her. Eye's slightly too wide, iris' almost too bright.

The figure cocked their head to the side and smirked. "So, what's your question?"

"You're not Vera," Evelyn said. "Where is Vera?" Around her, snow fell in clumped snowflakes, sticking to her coat, weighing down her eyelashes.

"Is that what you would like to know?" The figure moved almost clumsy, like the body inhabited was not quite like its own. Evelyn poked her head over the well, a dark vortex, an inescapable black hole.

"No," she paused. "I don't think so." The figure looked at her peculiarly. "I want enough wisdom to keep mother happy." A smile broke on the figures face, pointed, unlike the milk teeth still clouding Vera's smile.

"The deed is done, the price is paid," the figure said, its form quivering slightly around the edges. In the distance she could hear her mother's voice, calling them for dinner.

"The berry was a good payment then?" Evelyn asked.

"It's so cold," Vera's voice called from a distance. The figure smirked. Evelyn's stomach dropped. Suddenly, she didn't want Christmas dinner.

"Where's Vera," she asked.

"The payment was small compared to usual. But, its Christmas after all," the figure said.

CHRISTMAS: CANCELLED

by Holly Peters

The sight of the staggeringly tall Christmas tree with gaudy baubles in pink, purple, red and green made Bella flinch. The echo of a Christmas song spilled out of one of the shops surrounding the tight rows of uniform chairs. She looked over at Freddie who had slipped down the chair, his long legs stretched out in front of him and his head resting on the back of the seat. He had his earphones in and had a black woollen hat pulled down over his eyes. His chest slowly rising and falling with the serenity only granted by slept.

It infuriated her.

The screen of flights flashed from one page to another spanning across the globe, but each was followed by the same blurted word: cancelled.

Every time she read it, her stomach jolted like a rock dropped in the ocean.

A faceless voice filled the corners of the airport: "All flights cancelled – no flights scheduled for the rest of the day."

At the sound, some travellers filled with hope that was extinguished before it could even reach their cheeks. The others were numb to the announcement, staring into empty spaces or closing their eyes and imagining they were anywhere but there.

Freddy and Bella sat on their own row of plastic chairs, their luggage spilling out on the seat between them. For the last two hours, she'd sat typing on her laptop trying to pretend it was just any normal day and not Christmas eve.

It seemed every fifteen minutes the corner of her screen would blare with an alert of the storm.

They were calling it Storm Nicholas. Winds and rains across the world that had brought everything to a standstill: all planes planting their wheels firmly on the ground. Bella wondered *how many people would even notice?* So many would be spending the week indoors, glimmering Christmas lights replacing the stars that couldn't be seen in the sky.

***

Bella had stared out the taxi window on the drive to the airport, worried as the wheels plunged into craters of puddles and rain clattered on the roof like rattling tin cans. When she'd agreed to go on the trip, her boss had promised she'd be home for Christmas. *It was just a few music shows, an exciting adventure.* She had to do her job.

The window wipers were unable to keep up with the sheets of relenting water and it seemed it had a better way of showing her how she felt than she could articulate. But Freddy, as Freddy had been for the whole excruciating trip, just shrugged his shoulders and continued to scroll through his phone.

She looked at the sky heaving with sobs and could've sworn she could feel their pointed edges against her skin.

"What were you doing?" she barked.

"I lost track of time."

"That's your excuse for making us miss the only flight?" Another shrug.

For the rest of the drive, they sat trapped in a taut silence.

***

"So, where would you be if you weren't lucky enough to be stuck here with me?" Freddy asked pushing himself up the chair. He pulled the hat off his head and ran a hand through his messed hair.

Her fingertips hovered above the keys of her laptop, suspended. His voice had startled her – he wasn't usually one for conversation. She took a deep breath.

In the airport with the white walls and linoleum floor, it was like the storm had never happened. A pocket of shelter away from nature's roar. No hint of it except for the handfuls of tired travellers and the long list of flights that were supposed to be.

"As in how I would be spending my Christmas if I wasn't stuck chaperoning a moody popstar?"

"That's what I asked."

"Well…" She ducked the lid of her glaring laptop screen and placed it on the seat beside her.

"Probably would've just finished dinner and be shouting over a boardgame."

"With Christmas jumpers and cracker hats?"

"The only Christmas attire there is," she said. The feeling of shock she'd been sheltering all day finally morphed into sadness. "My grandad would be asleep by now and my sister's kids would be exhausted. Mum would be trying to convince us to drink her homemade eggnog instead of any of the nice drinks bought from the shop."

She quickly wiped her face, suddenly transported back across the ocean into a cold and uncomfortable airport seat with someone she'd only known for a week.

"Anyway, what would your Christmas look like?"

116

"Not much merrier than this," he said fiddling with a loose thread on the sleeve of his check shirt. He didn't offer anything else and Bella knew better than to push him. She could almost see the chest of memories he was desperate to force shut.

He raised himself up, the chair squeaking beneath him. He reached his arms overhead and without any words, walked off in the direction of the retail counters. The bright colours and competing smells almost gave her a headache even though she was sat so far away. She watched him go, then reached for her laptop slowly closing the documents that she had been repeatedly interrogating for the majority of Christmas eve.

She relaxed into the white noise, letting her shoulders roll down her back.

It had only been moments, but when she opened her eyes again Freddy was looming over her seat. She stared up at him, her face etched as a question mark. He was holding a turkey and stuffing sandwich with a small slice of fruit cake. A nervous look played on his cheeks.

"What's that?" Bella asked.

"It's Christmas dinner," he replied, "take it."

She grasped the food, feeling a low rumble rolling her stomach. She smiled slightly, but as she ripped the plastic film open, she could feel the weight of the gesture.

"Before you eat it, we have to do the cracker." Freddy pulled an envelope out of his pocket that had been twisted at both ends, something in the centre bulging.

"What is that?" she laughed reaching for the end he offered out to her.

"Don't laugh, I worked hard on this," he said. It was like an apology he was still practising to say.

"Thank you, Freddy."

"Merry Christmas Bella."

Printed in Great Britain
by Amazon

11240266R00078